Chronicles of an Ancient Forest

by John Christian

John Christian

Illustrations by Bernard Kear

First published 2001 by Magpie Publishing, Five Magpies, Elton, Newnham, Gloucestershire GL14 1JN

ISBN 0 9535672 1 4

Printed in Great Britain by M D Jenkins Printers Ltd., Units 53/54, Lydney Industrial Estate, Harbour Road, Lydney, Gloucestershire GL15 4EJ

INTRODUCTION

If you are so young as to recognise the Forest of Dean as it now is, only partly emerged but not yet irrevocably changed from its past, you may, among these chapters get some flavour of the old place. If, on the other hand, you are sufficiently old , you may get pleasure from having the strings of nostalgia plucked.

In seeking a title, the word *Chronicles* seemed to fit the idea of time. With this in mind I set the book into four chapters. The first deals with historical accounts. The next two chapters cover personal recollection, firstly from childhood and inevitably embracing the war years, and secondly from the times I worked in the forestry, or what was then called the Crown. The final chapter comprises of two stories, based on and adapted from incidents I had heard or read about.

In the complete annals of the ancient forest with its history and pre-history going right back to the nomadic hunter-gatherers who came to this place after the Ice Ages, these offerings are mere gleanings, a medley of random bits, brought together in the hope of touching your sense of entertainment. I am humble therefore in their sparsity and their presentation.

There is also added value. This takes the form of the wonderful illustrations compiled and drawn by Bernard Kear. When I handed him my manuscript I knew from his previous works that essence of the Forest of Dean came out of the end of his pencil. But I was unprepared for the excitement of seeing my writings brought to life as if he had been there, pulling out the words and fashioning them into living images. Some of the characters even look like the characters they were supposed to depict. The detail, the accuracy is astonishing. No pencil stroke seems random. Look at a plant and it is a foxglove or a fern and it is a hart's tongue; look for snipe in the marsh below Quarry Hill; look for work-creases in the clothes of the people and in the face of the old miner fishing. It's all there to tell it like it was. In Bernard Kear's drawings there is everything that is the Forest and I am very privileged to have had the attention of his discerning eye.

There used to be printed in old fictional novels, a disclaimer which ran something like this, "All the characters in this book are fictitious and do not on any account refer to persons living or dead." I considered this aspect carefully. Here was a dilemma. Did I consult a libel lawyer? Did I take out a hefty insurance against libel? Here, surely is the great problem with any form of biographical writing. In the end I decided I just had to take a chance. My disclaimer is simply, "This work is offered in loving esteem, an emotional act of sacred respect for those I describe. If there is humour it is a kind, full-throated laugh, never a snigger."

The characters of this book are or were my fellow Foresters, many were my companions at school and at work. I dedicate these writings to them with the utmost respect and understanding. Many of their names are included in my acknowledgement on the final page. If I have omitted any in print they are, nevertheless in my thoughts.

John Christian
September 2001

DEDICATED TO MY FRIEND IN
THE FOREST OF DEAN

Chapter 1

HISTORY

THE MYSTERIOUS DISAPPEARANCE OF SIR JOHN WINTER

To the good people of the North Forest the name Sir John Wyntour may be little more than of passing interest. This is because, in the passage of time, he has been reduced to the status of a squire of Lydney. In truth he and his family cast gigantic shadows, not merely on the history of Dean as a whole but on that of the nation too.

The Wintours as they were first called, came to Lydney in the reign of Henry VIII in or about 1543. The first John Wintour - mostly spelled with an 'i' - was a merchant adventurer and an entrepreneur in every sense of the word. Not only was he trading by sea as far afield as the Middle East, but he was sufficiently astute - exploitative perhaps! - to buy up the lands and associated business interests of the newly suppressed monastries.

The first John Wintour gave rise to four generations who succeeded him in Lydney before the family estates finally passed, by purchase, from the widow of the last squire, Sir Charles, to the Bathurst family in 1723.

This first John Wintour acquired immense social stature and prestige as a mariner. His brigs were trading Forest wool, cloth and iron in Spain and the Levant, returning to Lydney Pill with silk, fruit and wine. His activities reflect how great and rare were the resources of the Forest on the global market.

His offspring, too, impressed their status upon the nation and the Royal courts of Henry, Elizabeth and the Stuarts. They were sailors through and through; they were sea dogs of the truest pedigree. Their immense knowledge of seafaring was acquired through their trading adventures. These were days of fights with notorious Barbary pirates and Turkish slavers. There was an Errol Flynn in every one of these Wintour progeny!

William Wintour, John's second son, succeeded his father at Lydney. He was by then such a seasoned mariner that he became one of the prime influences in the formation of Henry VIII's new navy - the very first English Navy. Francis Drake, no less, was one of William's proteges. At one stage Drake lived at Gatcombe, Raleigh at Purton and Wintour at Lydney - a remarkable concentration of naval power about the Lower Severn!

William was duly knighted by Queen Elizabeth for his loyal services. He died in 1589 having been active and powerful in Lydney and in the nation as a whole for over thirty years! His son Edward took over from him and it seems then that the spelling of the family name changes to Wyntour. More recently it has become Winter.

Change there was too in the tenor of interests. Edward Wyntour was not so much a mariner as a technologist in iron. He constructed a small experimental forge at Whitecross House, the mansion of creamy Bath stone his father had erected just a little way out of Lydney along the Chepstow road. The site and the manorship of Lydney had previously been purchased from the Earl of Pembroke. Whitecross was to become the power-house of John Wyntour, Edward's son, during the harrowing days of the Civil War.

Edward died in 1619 and our Sir John Wyntour, the character this tale is leading up to, inherited his estate.

* * * * * * * * * * * *

It was a day in September 1664 in the English Civil War. Sir John Wyntour was fighting for his life on the rocky promontory at Beachley. His men had been surprised while engrossed in building a quay and a rapid communication route from Beachley Point over the River Wye towards Raglan Castle. But his sworn enemy, the Roundhead commander at Gloucester, Colonel Massey descended upon him without warning. A desperate and bloody action ensued and Wyntour's Royalists were routed. Sir John himself narrowly escaped, the legend is, by leaping off the 200 foot precipice at Woodcroft into the River Wye. The spot ever since, has been known as Wyntour's Leap.

The whole story fits with Sir John's historical reputation as a gallant and swashbuckling Cavalier. It might be said that in an historical Hollywood film his part might well have been played by Roger Moore or Harrison Ford - according to the preference of your age!

But this heroic figure wasn't all there was to Sir John. He is regularly vilified as the bogeyman of Dean, a man who fell short of being a carpetbagger only because he was a resident there. He is accused by most, though excused by some, as having exploited the resources of the Dean to the point of destruction without heart or thought for the people living there.

His excusers say this is nonsense and that he was a man of great constancy. He never proceeded they say, beyond his entitlements. He was beloved of many an influential person including Mr Pepys who referred to him fondly in his diaries. These beguilements say little about the the extreme nature of Sir John's entitlements.

Be that as it may, John Wyntour made much profit out of the Dean and his contracts with Kings Charles I and later, Charles II.

There is rather a prophetic record in a communication his grandfather William had once sent to a Royal Commission. This responded to the command for a ruthless search for vagabonds purporting to be terrorising the district. It stated he had found, "none but such beggarly, poor persons as are not thought fit to trouble your lordship with." Such was the status of the residents of Dean in the context of land rights!

No, Sir John's family and no doubt Sir John himself, were far from being philanthropists.

He is described by one source as "Ironmaster and Silviculturalist", and this just about sums up his enigmatic personality. In terms of the times these two pursuits were directly opposed to each other. The smelting of iron, the technology of which was still primitive, required woodsfull of timber in the form of charcoal. A silviculturalist serving such needs required to be a miracle worker! The historical records available make it clear that the constant demand for timber in the smelting of iron resulted in the denudation of the Dean of mature timber, by consequence reducing it to a wilderness of coppice. By the end of Sir John's time there was imperative need for an intense replanting programme and the creation of the great Georgian oak stands was finally introduced.

No, "silviculturalist" is a bit optimistic!

Sir John seems to have traded his family's status in seafaring for the technology of iron smelting. He did some very good deals with Charles I providing the King with much-needed revenue while feathering his nest tenfold and at the same time developing an awesome court status. He came to own virtually the whole of the Dean and its resources - in fact all, save the people in it!

He was almost the same age as Charles I but he was also an ardent Catholic - an irony, bearing in mind his grandfather's earlier grabbing of dispossessed monastry holdings!

Now being a Catholic in those times was a very chancy business and there was an implied loss of privilege.

Sir John's allegiance was in truth, to the Queen who was also of course unswervingly Catholic. John Wyntour was intensely loyal and gallant to her. He gave his personal protection to her retinue when she fled to Cornwall and thence to France in the anticipation of Charles's arrest. He served her throughout her life and even arranged her funeral. It seems therefore, it may have been the Queen rather than the Pope that stirred him.

In post-Henry VIII's Protestant nation, Catholic sympathies were in distinct disfavour. Moreover - and the mind boggles - there had been three Wyntours intimately involved in the Gunpowder Plot! All were executed! Nevertheless, Sir John Wyntour, until the Civil War at least, prospered both in private life and at Court. Bill Clinton had nothing on him! He continued to be a survivor in spite of desperate odds. He was forced to flee into exile, lost all his estates, was assigned to the Tower for four years. Still he came back! Little wonder he was able to jump off a 200 foot cliff mounted on his horse - and still come up trumps!

Came the Civil War and it was time to stand up and be counted. It was said the Roundheads were right and bad and the Cavaliers were wrong and good! That is obviously a simplification but it seems to be the popular view of the War - these dashing, plume-hatted, swashbuckling Cavaliers against the dour, crop-headed, fanatical Roundheads..

Sir John Wyntour was an active Cavalier. He operated with his own militia in what was the sort of buffer-zone of the Dean. Wales was considered wholly Royalist with defensive strongpoints along the borders and up the Wye at Chepstow, Monmouth and Goodrich. The Parliamentarians under Colonel Massey operated from Gloucester. There were many bloody skirmishes in the Dean which formed a sort of no-man's land between the two. Wyntour became Massey's sworn enemy - a personal encounter which finally ended up in confrontation at Lydney itself on the site of the fortified Whitecross House. Wyntour, rather than surrender his mansion to Massey, burnt it down and fled. At the dispossession of Charles, Massey received much of Wyntour's assets. Wyntour however, had the last laugh. Upon the

"I plunge down the scrubby slope above the precipice holding hard to the bridle of my nag… sliding, tumbling, not knowing where I would end up, fearing at any moment I would slide over the edge to the rocks below."

Restoration of the monarchy, Wyntour - wonder of wonders - got most of it back! Such was his influence at Court.

But we must go back to the skirmish at Beachley which happened when Wyntour and Massey were at their most aggressive height in order to finish relationships between this particular story.

Imagine we went there as reporters and in due course, had been able to interview all the protagonists in turn.

Sir John might have said:

"The action had gone badly for us. Surprised and outnumbered, the Roundheads fell upon us. A number of my men were sabred and quite a few took to the river whereupon they were swept away in the tide. But we nearly got Massey and would have killed him had not my man's carbine misfired!

"I was forced to retreat. Seizing a lance and mounting my steed I sped as fast as I could up the St Briavels road towards the woods. But ere I got far - Gadzooks! - I was cut off by several of Massey's men on horseback. I managed to elude them until, upon reaching the sheer cliffs of the Wye, I saw them converging upon me from several directions. An officer shouted, 'That's Wyntour! Pistol him!'

"My own weapon is discharged; I have only a broken pike. The ravine is behind me. Massey's men are charging down on me. There is no time. I plunge down the scrubby slope above the precipice holding hard to the bridle of my nag, steadying us with the shaft of the pike, sliding, tumbling, not knowing where I would end up, fearing at any moment I would slide over the edge to the rocks below! Suddenly, and to my great surprise, I realise my unchecked progress has brought me to a wide ledge extending horizontally along the face of the cliff - quite broad enough, in fact, to lead a horse along.

"This ledge is obscured from above by a cornice of rocks and in its length by thick bushes and scrub. It is, to all intents and purposes, invisible to Massey's men. I can hear them riding back and forth above the cliff shouting and crying, 'Find him! Find him!' The fools think naught to dismount and give the area the benefit of a thorough scrutiny. After some time they seem to have ridden off up the St Briavels road thinking I have perhaps made my way towards my place at Lancaut. I am able to proceed along the ledge which is remarkably wide and secure. I suddenly emerge into some bland pastures above the Wye. The hue and cry has passed on. I have no

difficulty in scrambling down to the river and swimming across, uttering fervent thanks to the great mercy of God, and eventually making my way to the security of Raglan."

On the other hand, a conversation with a trooper who had been amongst those who pursued Wyntour towards the Wye revealed the following:-

"Well - in confidence mind - we lost the swine when we should 've 'ad 'im. Our officer 'o 'ad seen 'im before, recognised 'im. There 'e was with only a broken pike an' we all gallopin' 'ard at 'im. 'E couldn't go nowhere 'cause the gorge drops away in a great precipice. But when you're on 'orseback an' 'ave to make sure the animal don't stumble in its eagreness you 'ave to take yer eye off the quarry. When we got to the spot where 'e'd bin standin' - there wus nothin'! - not a bloody thing! Everyone wus shoutin' and the'officer a'ravin'!

"I reckon Wyntour'd found a way over the edge 'an we might 'ave 'eard 'im crashin' down if we'd bin sensible enough to keep quiet. But there it was. We knew the Colonel'd 'ave no mercy when 'e learned we'd lost 'im.

"Amos Jones come up to me an' whispered, 'That's 'im 'en it? - Down there, drownin' in the river.'

"I looked down an' couldn't see nothin'.

"'Down there,' said Amos, pointin' an' winkin' an' nudgin' me in the ribs.

"Well, I soon cottoned on an' we swore it.

"Later, one or two expanded on this story an' said they saw Wyntour on 'is 'orse fleein' from us when 'e come to the gorge. Without a second thought over 'e went - nag an' all! It wus obvious 'e wusn't goin' to survive.

"Unfortunately fer us, the Captain come up to us a few days later. Colonel Massey was with 'im lookin' daggers! 'You men - you saw Wyntour drowning didn't you?.'

"'Yes sir," says Amos. 'Well the pig's turned up in Newport - as fit and treasonable as ever!'

"We couldn't believe it!

"'You saw him virtually dead, with his horse, in the river after falling 200 feet or more, did you not?'

"Amos gulps. "Why yes sir - no doubt about it.'

"The Captain 'e looks at me an' then at William Phelps an' at Ephraim James, each in turn, as fierce as a 'awk.

"Well, we cannot deny it can us? An' there's nothin' like the fear of a floggin' to make the expression of a lyin' man more sincere. We say in unison, "Yes sir. No doubt about it. 'E were doomed.'

"The Captain looks relieved an' turns to the Colonel. 'You see sir. Absolutely no question. My men wouldn't lie on pain of death!' The Colonel nods. 'The swine has a charmed life, Gadzooks' he says with some heat.

"We 'eard afterwards 'e'd told the yarn about Wyntour's miraculous escape at a regimental dinner attended by Lord Cromwell no less!

"No wonder the myth was perpetuated and was written into 'istory!

"Ol' Amos an' me splits our sides w'en we talks about it!"

* * * * * * * * * * * *

Now you may think, dear Reader, that all this is pure fanciful speculation. But I assure you that running along the face of the cliff above the river, is a wide ledge, proceeding safe and secure, until it emerges into bland fields. At least it was when I was there nearly twenty years ago.

The story is of one of the Dean's best and most dramatic legends. You can go and see Wyntour's Leap quite easily. It is hard by the road - a kind of grotto, opening immediately from the road itself, unmarked and easily missed, distinguished only by a council litter bin. Walk a few paces and you are looking down into the serpentine coils of the river 200 cool feet below.

Research: "Wyntours of White Cross" Frank H. Harris. 1923.
"Four Personalities from the Forest of Dean" Ralph Anstis. 1996.

FOREST WILDLIFE

The wretched and sickening incident of the Ruardean bears was enacted close to Dunk's Corner and in any case has featured so prominently in Forest recent history that it may not be ignored here. Many of the family names of those I went to school with were those of the bears incident and indeed, my own maternal family of Baldwin supplied two of the miscreants!

I have to confess that my first approach to the story of the Ruardean bears was a joky one. My intended review of the affair was laced with jocular ideas like the suggestion of establishing a Ruardean *Bear* Festival! - or changing the name of one of the Ruardean inns to *The Dancing Bears* - and so on. After all, time is a great healer and humour a great dispeller of tragedy. The Gloucestershire poet F W Harvey included the Ruardean incident in his comic poem about the Forest; he was no stranger to the realities of violence and its more sombre aspects on the Western Front.

A man there was, a gentle soul,
Of mild enquiring mind,
Who came into this neighbourhood
Its wonders for to find.

. . . .

Until one sleepy summer's eve
He came all unaware
Unto a place called Ruardean
And asked 'Who killed the bear?'

The men arose and punched him flat
Another punched his head,
And when the rest had done with him,
Our gentle friend was dead.

The moral of this simple tale
Is plain, Dear Friend, beware,
If you should visit Ruardean
Mention of any bear!

But having got into the detail of the thing and read what was left of the reports of the Court proceedings, I had to admit that it was indeed a baleful affair, an example of uncouth and primitive behaviour even for that day and age. The main defence is that it had no rationality. It was an aberration amongst a tough but kindly people. I became convinced that the matter was, as most people seemed to agree, best relegated to the annals of obscurity and lost in the mists of time. This process has in fact, already begun. The Court Minute Book for 1898 for instance, is missing, the copies of press accounts are so dog-eared that whole chunks are gone. Neither is there any person any longer alive who is able to give even second-hand witness.

I asked the lady at the shop in Ruardean, if I should go into The Angel and enquire loudly at the bar, *"Who killed the bears?"*? Would I get a helping of knuckle pie? She replied probably no one would know what I was talking about!

It is true that at the time of the incident there was general revulsion. In its comment column *The Mercury* intoned, *"The Forest will be considered the abode of primal savages."*

Here was the crux of it all. The Forest and its people as a whole, were labelled wild and barbarous. At the same time however, Ruardean itself objected to becoming the scapegoat for the sins of a few.

So I have decided there is no justification, no purpose in resurrecting all the details in yet another laboured description. I merely offer some pertinent comments.

The two dancing bears were cruelly slaughtered and their French owners severely beaten by a mob incensed by the totally untrue rumour that the animals had killed a child and scarred a woman for life. Who started the rumour and why, is now largely irrelevant. Exactly where it all started and who was involved has preoccupied many simply because of the sneaking conviction that the good people of Ruardean village near where the climax to the events occurred, had in truth, nothing at all to do with it. There are no doubts that those charged and convicted came chiefly from Ruardean Hill not Ruardean village itself, a fact which has great importance in terms of Forest parochialism.

The accused were in the main colliers and according to one of the French witnesses, had black faces; one may conclude they had therefore just come off early shift, straight as it were, from the pit.

The main fracas was said to have started near the junction of two roads, one to Ruardean and one to Drybrook.

The one bear was killed with an eagerness that a mob might be expected to exhibit and in the heat of the moment. The second was more rationally dispatched. The first attempt to do so was made, not it seems by one of those charged, but by a man who said he wanted, *"to put the animal out of its misery."* Significantly, he was not charged. A shot failed to kill this bear - but another man who cut the animal's throat WAS charged! By this time, this second bear had run to Marstow Farm a mile beyond Ruardean village, in deep countryside and, one might conclude, beyond the worst excesses of mob hysteria.

If you read what is left of the available press reports and the few allegedly true accounts, many contradictions appear.

Witnesses do not seem to agree where the killings occurred. One says the smaller bear was struck down on the open road, *"within sight of the village."* Another says it was outside *Mason's shop*, presumably premises in the village itself.

One of the Frenchmen said the attacks began, *"on the outskirts of Cinderford."* In another statement he says they began near two pubs. The two pubs were likely to have been *The Old Engine* and *The Mitre* both in Steam Mills, confused by the writer Leonard Clarke in an account written in 1981, as *The Engine* and *The Old Inn* which he claimed existed in the vicinity of Cinderford.

The main fracas was said to have started near the junction of two roads, one to Ruardean and one to Drybrook. This sounds like Nailbridge but it could conceivably have been farther up the Morse Road at the bottom of The Hollow between *The Nelson Inn* and *The Rose and Crown.*

Even the names of the Frenchmen were corrupted. *The Mercury* report of the Court proceedings gives them as Gabriel Qugant Tah, Gabriel Baluit Hugent, Thomas Sergaint and Alfred Gerand, as unlikely a collection of names as you might encounter!

It's a rum business all round.

The young men of Ruardean Hill seem to have been incited by an inn keeper. Their rage was, on the face of it, engendered by a drunken rumour - but they were not to know since the drunks had long since staggered home to sleep off their inebriation.

There seems to have been an element of racism in the mob's actions. One witness said, *"The English were chasing the French."* which polarises the matter a little beyond a mere local skirmish. The memories of the Napoleonic Wars were still in the local consciousness - and the French were still the foe:

> *"We byut thay at Wayterloo, didn' us?"!*
> So no quarter for the enemy!

As for the bears, here were men - colliers - used to a kind regard for their pit ponies, tough men who had no need to take out hate on dumb animals. One has to remember too, that they had literally just come out of the pit - not a rational world with rational rules but a black, harsh one with different values and violent death just around the corner. Disorientation in a world of light, where a dastardly crime, the killing of a child, had taken precedent over all else was likely to have received distorted judgement.

Perhaps that is being too kind; a psychological excuse. But I reckon that had a first class counsel been on hand to represent the accused, he would have had them all discharged, if not on points of law, on confused and circumstantial evidence and mitigating circumstances.

Finally and ironically, had the incident of the bears happened today, the outcome might not have been so very much different. The Frenchmen would have been attacked, not by local youths but by animal rights extremists. The bears, having been freed by the mob would have undoubtedly been officially shot by a police marksmen on a point of public safety!

That might be a cynical summing-up but it puts the thing in the right perspective. In that right perspective, by sleight of hand, the infamous affair might thankfully be disappeared off the face of history.

Research:

Leonard Clark: "Who killed the Bears".
pub. Forest of Dean Newspapers Ltd. 1981.

Press Reports and Summaries: Dean Forest Mercury, Friday, May 3rd 1889.
F W Harvey. Poem "Warning" from, "In Pillowell Woods".
Pub. Frank Harris. 1926.

The names of the Frenchmen were given as Gabriel Qugant, Gabriel Hugent, Thomas Sergaint and Alfred Gerand

THE ANCIENT HIGHROAD

The ancient highroad running through the Forest from Gloucester to Monmouth is described by that excellent historian the Rev. H G Nicholls as following a line which, in the course of history, has rarely deviated from its present route. It was along this route for instance, that the Royalist Lord Herbert, led his army of 500 horse and 1500 foot on to Gloucester in 1643. Today it is the A4136.

This road, until the end of the 18th century, was the only trans-Forest route proceeding westward into the Wye Valley at Monmouth. Another main route from the east, now the A4151, came in from Elton, rising up a steep, preordained route to Littledean, then turning northward to join the A4136 at Dunks Corner. It was as if the A4151, reaching the 800 foot ridge above Cinderford and having visibility of the huge expanse of unbroken forest stretching away to Hart Hill in the far distance above the Wye, decided to turn away, back to less primitive lands! But the route did not in fact end above Cinderford. Less fearful souls proceeded onwards towards Speech House and the centre of the forest. A lesser road, now the B4226 plunged down the long steep hill at St Whites to wind its way through to Coleford, gradually converging with the A4136 until the two joined at the Long Stone between Coleford and Staunton - surely a matter of no coincidence?

We have all been told many times, how dire used to be the isolation of the Forest, how poor were the roads and how primitive were the few inhabitants. But it takes some special concentration of the imagination to appreciate the extreme of these conditions, right up to 1800 when, at the same time, Bristol and London basked in splendid elegance. England was about to give up the slave-trade but many cities were wealthy with the gains; a time just before the Battle of Waterloo; a time the great grandfathers of present octogenarians might just have known.

This imbalance was all to do with communication of course. Run of the mill people did not come to the Forest for the simple reason that, not only was it off the beaten track, but it was difficult to penetrate. The few roads to and through it, were churned up by coal and timber limbers. The lesser roads were little more than woodland tracks. The Forest was a good place to hide, a bad and often dangerous one to visit. It was indeed, a place to be exceptionally avoided.

Nicholls, in his book *Forest of Dean,* gives a dramatic description which concentrates the perception on the primitive Dean of the time. It is, he said, a place of discontinence, *"those paths which penetrated its depths, having their direction turned and rendered perplexing through the frequent interposition of streams, bogs and thickets. Such were the means of communication which for many generations served the purposes of the Foresters, who permitted no wheeled vehicles to enter their domain and possessed few if any themselves."* This of course applied to the branch roads. But the major ones were equally unacceptable because they were under constant degradation from the haulage of minerals or timber, rendering them virtually impassable to lighter traffic in winter.

The industrialisation of the Dean which, even before the Indutrial Revolution proper, had been premeditated by mining and smelting, made it critical that the road system be improved. A Roads Act in 1795 demanded improvements of the Forest roads and it was after this date but only during the first half of the 1800s that extensive improvements were achieved.

In the case of the ancient Gloucester to Monmouth road as it traverses the Forest, Dunk's Corner is the first of four very strategic points. The next is at Mirey Stock where junctions lead off to the South Forest and Lydney Docks and also northward to Lydbrook and the Wye Valley. The third is at Five Acres where branches spread out to West Dean. The fifth is the afore described confluence of the present A4136 and the B4226 (westward progression of the A4151) near the Long Stone.

If you wanted to penetrate the Dean from the northeast on horseback or by carriage you came from the direction of Westgate Bridge at Gloucester, the first downstream crossing of the Severn. Earlier on, if you were a Roman, a Celt or you were trading in iron or timber by sea, you probably came from Chepstow or from Lydney Docks direction. You might even have come up the river as far as Newnham.

For travellers therefore, these two main in-routes through Mitcheldean on the one hand and Littledean on the other were all important, as in fact, they still are today.

It is with a sense of surprise, that one learns, for a short period after 1795, the section of the ancient route through Mitcheldean was discarded in favour of an alternative one leading into the town, from there up and over Stenders Hill to Drybrook, rejoining the old route at Dunk's Corner. This was done because this new route, as described by Nicholls, *"ascended the Stenders Hill by a more even slope avoiding the abrupt rise of Harrow Hill."* The Forest

In between were steep outcrops of the Pennant Sandstone and the marshy bottom of the Dry Brook to overcome - a sort of Scylla and Charybdis dilemma!

Church and Nicholls's vicarage were situated alongside the Harrow Hill route. Can Nicholls ever have got over to see the Stenders one?!

For those who travel the two alternatives today, the distinction in terms of gradient seems inconceivable. The fierce drag up the Stenders Hill is far, far steeper than anything Harrow Hill can offer. But two considerations are at work here. Firstly, the severity of the ancient route is contained on the Plump Hill side of Harrow Hill where the road toils over the eastern escarpment of the Dean syncline, up past the site of the old Point Inn and through what is now ground made up from quarry waste and iron mining. Secondly, on the descent from the top of Harrow Hill (I use here the name Harrow Hill because Nicholls uses it) a fairly hazardous profile probably existed on that stretch between the site of the Forest Church on Quarry Hill on one side and the lower spur of Ruardean Hill at Hawkwell on the other. In between were steep outcrops of the Pennant Sandstone and the marshy bottom of the Dry Brook to overcome - a sort of Scylla and Charybdis dilemma!.

Reading Nicholls, it seems that it was not until 1841 that the route from Dunkley's Corner to Mitcheldean was improved, perhaps by using quarry and mine waste and introducing loops to ease gradients. It is likely that during these latter improvements the great, raised causeway carrying the modern road from the Forest Church graveyard to Dunk's was constructed. This took away the need to descend through the marshy lands of Gorebrook to the east of the vicarage and the subsequent valley of the brook. From then on it seems the traffic preferred the Plump route to the Stenders one.

Between all these considerations one detects an interesting story of entrepreneurianism!

On September 5th 1796, James Graham, the proprietor of the George Inn at Mitcheldean sought fit to place an advertisement in the Gloucester Journal. In it he first of all extends *"respectful thanks"* to those who gave him *"liberal support."* Just whom he thanks and for what purpose is not made clear!

He then announces to the public, *"The new road through His Majesty's Forest of Dean, leading from Mitcheldean through Coleford and Monmouth ... is already greatly improved and in short will be equal to any in this part of the country. It is allowed that travellers will save a mile at least by taking this way from Gloucester to Monmouth. Graham has laid in a stock of admirable port and other wines and every exertion will be made for public accommodation." He adds rather significantly, "Post chaises at 1s per mile, and sober drivers."* - the drivers were presumably barred from the admirable port!

It is construed Mr Graham had powerful pals and by dint of persistent lobbying perhaps, he had managed to change the route of the main road to run past his hostelry!

The mile that the detour claims to have saved is interesting. Was here an early case of advertising misrepresentation? A look at the modern roads on the ordnance survey maps, the one over the Stenders, the other over The Plump, seemingly show no advantage in distance; in fact the former is perhaps even a little longer. Both routes merge at Dunk's. If Nicholls is correct, that the Plump route *"remained nearly identical with the present line"* then the mile claimed by Mr Graham saved on the Stenders route is optimistic.

The Stenders preference seems to have persisted over a period from 1796 until 1841 during which time it did much for the welfare and commerce of Mitcheldean. Subsequently however, a tollgate built at Dunk's gave returns showing that well over twice as many travellers were using the Plump route over the Stenders one. (It is interesting, at the same time, to note that it was in 1841 that a good route was constructed from Nailbridge to Bishop's Wood where the Wye crossing at Goodrich was available over Kerne Bridge. There was a toll at Dunk's and one at Kerne Bridge. The latter was still in operation in the 1930s when I used to pay an old penny - or was it a halfpenny - to take a bicycle across.)

So Dunk's Corner is a relatively modern place after all. The Railway Inn, long gone, would have been constructed some time after 1810 coinciding with that of the railway branch line to Drybrook. Its landlord would have served the trickle of travellers proceeding along what was to become the A4136, on foot, on horseback or by carriage towards Monmouth. This trade would have been outstripped by the thirsty nail-makers and quarrymen and later the coalminers who were intensely busy about this area.

All along the Nailbridge valley on both sides, are quarries, now secret and overgrown, homes to jackdaws and kestrels, stock doves and pied wagtails, which were our adventure playgrounds as children in the 1930s. Above them crowded the Georgian oakwoods and seas of bracken in which to play *'ares 'n 'ounds*. Alice Jordan's garden teetered above a fearful, quarried abyss filled with black, unfathomable water. Long-since abandoned mines were everywhere into which one could creep or down which one could lower candles in jam-pots until the flame glimmered on dank and dripping planks and on which ancient sheep fleeces, green with age, from lost members of the flock, were draped. Shaded ponds lay in secret places where huge, orange-bellied newts could be stalked and caught in home-made nets.

What more could a child want?!

Research: Rev. H G Nicholls, MA. "Forest of Dean." Pub. Macmillan 1858.

Chapter 2

THE WAR, BEFORE & AFTER

THE MILKMAN GETS A HANGUP

Guy Fawkes' Night was always well-celebrated in the Forest - not perhaps because of any particular animosity towards the old Papist; more because there was always a plentiful supply of natural material available for huge bonfires. Dead bracken makes a spectacular blaze sending up showers of incandescent sparks like a giant firework in its own right. In those carefree days when the sacrifice of an odd eye or finger unreasonably seemed a fair price to pay for the fun, most families had their individual bonfire. Such a scene is of course totally unacceptable today and would earn the gravest reproof from a host of organisations - from the Fire Brigade to ROSPA and back again. As a result we now congregate in tidy groups and watch sanitized displays put on by clever and safety-wise experts; off stage, energy-saturated youth finds more wilful and lethal ways to do the body damage!

No, Guy Fawkes was an institution. Guys were trailed around on makeshift trolleys for days beforehand. Tinder may have been plentiful but burnable clothes were quite hard to come by because most were assigned to the purpose of work until they literally fell to bits. Nevertheless, tattered jackets and trousers tied at the sleeves and legs, were begged, borrowed and stolen. Stuffed with dead bracken and topped with a potato bag and cap, they made a very life-like and combustable Guy.

In those pre-war days milk was delivered to the doorstep "loose" as it were, in a galvanized churn, measured into the waiting jugs with dinky, little, brass-stamped measures which were all hanging around the rim of the churn in regimental order from the smallest to

The figure, dressed in my father's old, grey suit a pair of brown brogues dangling disjointedly out of the legs, his faded, fawn trilby cocked almost jauntedly over one eye above grisly, sweat-encrusted hair, twitched wickedly. It gyrated from a thin rope which attached it to the trussed beam.

the largest. The milk came by pony and trap at an early but respectable hour - a cheerful adjunct to the start of the day.

The local milkman was a friend and an acquaintance to all, his face and his beaming demeanor a constant familiarity upon the scene. Joe Bower was our local milkman. He came early to our house. The milk jug was placed ready for him just inside the back-kitchen door and out of the way of the cats. Joe was a jolly character with a real liking for his trade and a disposition akin to a sunny morning. He would thump the door, throw it open while shouting a cheerful *"Milko!"* and, in the same motion, bend down towards his milk pail seizing the empty jug and carefully ladling the required amount of milk into it. The milk foamed with sheer freshness.

This operation was smooth, accomplished and highly satisfying to the looker-on. The measure swirled into the pail and came out brimming with creamy milk. This in turn was transferred lovingly into the jug with a caring, liquid motion difficult to put adequately into words. The pint measure might be followed by a half pint and so on, and always a bit for the cat! It was like pulling beer at a beer engine or ringing church bells or stroking a donkey's ears! It was something you just wanted to do! Many's the time I stood enthralled, watching the arrival of the milk, my mind thinking of sleek, contended cows, of green pastures dotted with cowslips, of man and beasts in a holy, joyful pact. Here to our milk jug was brought intrinsic goodness. Pasturisation? What was that when it was home?!

It was the morning of November 5th and Joe Bower went through his traditional motions. The only difference was something unusual caught on the retina of his eye as he made that bowing motion towards the pail.

My mother, busy in the kitchen next to the back-kitchen, listened to the familiar 'Milko' cry. It was followed not by the chinking of metal against the side of the churn, but a gasp followed by a whispered blasphemy she would rather not have heard. She ran to the door. There, leaning against the door-post was Joe, as white as his milk, his measure dangling listlessly from one hand. He was staring pop-eyed at a figure which appeared to be dancing in mid-air below one of the stout roof trusses. The figure, dressed in my father's old, grey suit a pair of brown brogues dangling disjointedly out of the legs, his faded, fawn trilby cocked almost jauntedly over one eye above grisly, sweat-encrusted hair, twitched wickedly. It gyrated from a thin rope which attached it to the trussed beam.

Joe's legs seemed to be dissolving into a boneless jelly in danger of failing to support his sagging body. His eyes had retreated into their sockets like small, shrunken marbles.

My mother rushed to his aid. A strong grasp on his arm and shoulder propelled him to the wheelback chair standing in the corner. In the motion she elbowed the dangling figure roughly aside. The potato-bag face with its grinning, crayoned mouth, swayed into view. A little of the coco-fibre hair fell away.

Joe slumped. My mother said, *"Wait there, Joe. I'll get you a strong cup of tea."*

As she hurried to the hob she called, *"Arthur! How could you frighten Joe out of his skin. He thought you'd hanged yourself."* My father had not yet caught the bus to work.

My father, who had a rather devilish sense of humour, denied indignantly that there had been any ill-intent - but I noticed in the retelling of the story to various friends, the concern in his voice was replaced by a tendency to grin.

The hanged man was of course our guy in dad's old clothes, stuffed with bracken and hung up to dry. Joe Bower wasn't to know this. It took him a long time to get over the shock and he always said a feeling of doom persisted every time he pushed our back door open.

A TALE OF TWO BANANAS

At the top of the Plump Hill on Fairplay Green is a fishing pond, a relic of the derelict Westbury Brook Iron Mine. There one afternoon, an aged, retired collier, the ingrained, blue marks of the coal on his face and hands showing the history of his crippling work, sat, a decrepit cane rod propped in the notch of forked stick, two small roach on the bank beside him. The fish were blooded, the redness of the blood contrasting with the orange of their fins; they were intended for the pot. The old chap's float, a red and white goose quill, bobbed vigorously above a hook dressed with flour-paste bait.

"'Course thee cost yut 'em, my boy. Soak 'em in salt fust. Mind the bwuns, mind! But thay be awright wi' a bit a' bread an' butter."

A whole new vista of activity opened up before the two small boys who enviously regarded this scene. All one needed was a bean-stick, a length of black twine, a pin bent like a hook and a float made from a cork and of course, a tin containing a sticky mix of flour-and-water paste - *("a bit a sugar in it do attract 'em too.")*

Small boys and relatively deep ponds do not go well together. At best, wet feet and mud-filled boots (Wellingtons were rare!), were not condusive to parental peace. At worst - well, there had been tragedies.

Local ponds, the derelict remains of shut-down industry were distributed throughout the Forest. Clay-ridden, somewhat desolate trenches filled with muddy water and surrounded by trees, they supported a meagre variety of fish. There were some roach and perch but mostly a local strain of rather unbeautiful common carp. The Fairplay Pond was fortunate to have some nice roach.

One of the most off-putting features of these ponds was the inevitable presence of a dead dog.

It used to be, sad to say, the practice amongst some to get rid of their unwanted dog by drowning it. A brick tied about the neck and the animal cast into a local pond was the cruel fate for a dog that worried sheep or was

An aged, retired collier, the ingrained, blue marks of the coal on his face and hands showing the history of his crippling work, sat, a decrepit cane rod propped in the notch of forked stick, two small roach on the bank beside him.

savage. It may seem unthinkable but one has to remember that there is no easy way of putting down a wayward dog humanely if you have no money for the services of a vet or you do not possess a shotgun, as few did. The remains of these poor animals thus disposed of, eventually filled with gases to float, backside-up, to offend the eyes and nose in some dismal backwater avoided by fishermen.

That is by the way however. The two small boys who had witnessed the old collier's success had no qualms about the hazards. They determined to institute their own fishing expedition. It needed to be well-planned since parental objection was inevitable.

By consequence, at 5.30 of a fine Sunday morning, a small boy armed with a newly-constructed bean-stick rod and all the accompanying home-made parphernalia, lurked beneath the undergrowth opposite his friend's bungalow at Hawkwell.

The contact call - the hoot of an owl made through cupped hands - was given three times in all.

There was absolute silence from the blind, curtained windows giving no account of the drama occurring within. The minutes dragged by. The house remained sunk in the silence of an early, pre-War Sunday morning.

Three more hoots; not a murmur!

Then pandemonium erupted! The French doors onto the verandah - little-used ever - burst open outwards. Through the black cavity beyond the lace curtains, flew a small boy brandishing a bean-stick rod, catapaulted as it were, with fiendish force into that soft, summer morning. Immediately behind came a larger figure grasping hastily-tied pyjama trousers, in an attempt to deter their premature departure!

Small figure hits the lawn running, crosses the road in a shot and disappears into the surrounding vert! The crashing of bracken fronds, sounding less and less into the depths of the wood, is the only sign of the fugitive's erstwhile presence. The larger figure stops on the steps to the verandah. It raises its arm and shakes its fist. *"I'll get you, my lad! - and it'll be the strap for you!"* There was no concession to child rights in those days.

But the bird was flown!

At 9.00 am. father of number one small boy, leisurely taking advantage of the only morning of the week free of the need to get up for work, discovers son's bed to be empty. Much consternation since this is a departure from the normal, cosy advantages of home. There is no sign however, of what might lie behind the mysterious absence.

Time drags on.; 10 o'clock - 11 o'clock - no sign of departed offspring; noon and dinner under way!

Then a discovery is made. Two bananas have disappeared from the shelf in the pantry where they had previously reposed. Bananas speak of sustenance for journeys.

Father One sets out on peddle cycle to Father Two and learns of early-morning drama.

Much racking of brains to guage possible energy potential in terms of distance of two bananas. Fairplay Pond, a mile away, fits the bill.

At 1.00 pm. figure riding bike appears coming over hill to where two small boys sit on bankside - fishless but still determined. The bananas have long-since been devoured, their blackening skins being the only foreign objects on the bank beside the fishermen.

In those days the Point Inn, just a step or two down the Plump Hill below Fairplay Green, had a small shop attached to it, selling sweets and all sorts of bric-a-brac - including - simple cane fishing rods bearing a length of green twine, a proper red and white float and above all, a barbed hook.

Father, perhaps in relief at finding the lost adventurers, bought two such fishing kits and even forfeited his own traditional Sunday dinner to remain to supervise an hour of proper fishing.

The old Point Inn, like the Railway at Dunk's, is gone. Fairplay Pond is a minor nature reserve though fishing hopefuls may still be seen parked along the banks in summer. Woodlarks used to trill above the red mounds of Westbury Brook mining spoil which have now been smoothed into a comfortable series of picnicking nooks and dingles to which the woodlarks are unlikely to return. But fishing in the Dean has reached new heights of high technology and efficiency since we plied the roach of Fairplay with bent pins and flour paste, so we must move on.

In the immediate post-War period, during the late 1940s and 1950s, a new breeze blew. People were looking for ways and means to extend their lives. Leisure was still scarce - for instance, if you were lucky enough to get a paid holiday at all, it was a mere week. Travel was too expensive for most - and in any case, to what purpose? The benefit of the employee? The only benefit was the profit his employer made out of his labour. No labour, no profit! Paying for a holiday for your workmen was paying twice over! Concepts of a happy labour-force?! Christ Almighty!!

So there was no concept of leisure.

Deep in the psyche of Foresters lay an innate tendency to fish. Perhaps it was acquired way back in the days of hunter-gatherer ancestors. Frustrated by vast periods of their living days spent underground, hacking out the mineral deposits of the Earth, this latent urge finally emerged. Ageing ex-miners now with open space and the good Lord's skies above them instead of timber props and shale, would sit patiently on the bank of some clay-ridden, mud-pool, waiting to catch one or two of the small roach or carp that lived there.

The Forest pools were, as I have described, small, muddy and the spin-off of industrial activities. Their names reflected the pits that had spawned them - Lightmoor, Meadowcliff, Waterloo-Screens, Crabtreehill and so on. The Brickworks at Hawkwell and Marian's Brickworks at Staunton were other sites of piscatorial potential while Cannop Ponds, still mildly polluted, were there in potential only. Soudley Ponds were owned by a posh syndicate and restricted to fishing for trout with the fly. In Blackpool Brook, winding its way beneath venerable oaks from Fox's Bridge down to Blakeney, you might, with the knowhow, tickle a small trout (which grew in dimensions as the years surrounding its capture extended!). The River Lyd managed to support a few coarse fish of the moving-water variety but suffered the same pollution as Cannop Ponds. The Drybrook to Soudley Brook too suffered industrial and domestic pollution.

The Forest's anglers sat with their battered cane rods and quill floats, pleased perhaps to get continuous fresh air into their lungs rather than the clotting coal-dust of the pits. They did so without licence or permit, their undoubted right as Foresters unquestioned and unquestionable. The Forestry Commission, like Brer rabbit, stayed mum! What was a few casual and inconspicuous fishermen in the green-ness of all these woods?!

And so it was an incomer, a keen angler named John Hosking, who came to live near Littledean and was amazed and appalled at the intransigence of Foresters in the belief that they did not require organising on the fishing front, that set the wheels in motion towards an integrated angling scene!

A letter from John Hosking to the Forestry Commission eventually stimulated the latter to consider letting its fishing for what it was worth - which wasn't much! The Commission was, it advised, prepared to institute formal leases for the fishing of its waters, but to properly constituted clubs. John Hosking immediately put in hand the arrangements to constitute such a club. The word got round and next to no time, three angling clubs were vying for leases - Lydney, Yorkley and, in their majesty, the Royal Forest!

John Hosking was an incomer. What knew he of Forest traditions?! In the impasse which arose, Yorkley set their caps - or if you like, their rods - at Cannop Ponds, leaving the Royal Forest a mere hotch-potch of minor muddy puddles (several of which like Heron's Pool at Sling did not even exist any more as a potential fishery). The best was Lightmoor Pond near Cinderford. The next best, though by a great shortfall, Hawkwell Brickworks near Steam Mills. Crabtreehill Pond was a little-known crescent of stagnant water completely surrounded by the old spoil heaps of the disused colliery. Meadowcliff Pond was a well-fished but tiny pool on the site of that long-disused pit near Hawkwell. Waterloo Screens was a similar relic not far away from the last beyond Brierley and completely buried in the woods. Cannop Colliery Pond was on the opposite side of the road to the Lido and was a tiny bit of water completely overgrown. Marian's Brickworks out on the Monmouth road between Coleford and Staunton was a good carp pool but likely to be polluted by timber preservative leaking from the adjacent timber yard. Heron's Pond I have described. The Blackpool Brook, a tiny stream flowing from Crabtreehill through the heart of the Forest to Blakeney, was thrown in for good measure. This brook had trout - of tiny stature - but as to being a club water, it had no chance.

Lydney Club had its own long-established lake at Lydney Rec. and, so far as I remember, was offered, in addition, the first few miles of the River Lyd which had a head of small coarse fish.

Everyone was looking sideways at the other and sweet-mouthing the Forestry Commission officials! The Royal Forest sought to swallow the lot! The Forestry Commission sensing discord, played coy.

John Hosking proposed a meeting with Yorkley to discuss amalgamation. This meeting was convened at the Nagshead Inn at Yorkley - I don't know - some time back in the early 1960s. (The early minutes of the Royal Forest were subsequently lost.)

It began well enough, if edgy. Then Hosking, loosened by the effects of good Yorkley ale, suddenly said, *"Did you hear the one about the Forester who thought a mended kelt was a Welshman with his leg in a splint?!"*

The Royal Forest were lucky to get out without a taste of knuckle pie! Any ideas of amalgamation were rendered inoperable.

And so has the division of angling interests remained in the Forest ever since, but all disputes have their turning points. There is no longer any discord. The clubs became united in their battles against the loose canons, those who thought fishing should be free for all as a right. Notice boards were dug up and thrown in the water and when anchored out in the water were blasted with shotguns. Each club had to prove its right in the old-fashioned way. Gradually, this took place and rules were established.

Nowadays there is friendly inter-club competition. All the waters have been improved or extended and stocked. Angling in the Forest is now a magnificent and much supported activity. Forest anglers can hold their own against any aquatic based region.

It's a far cry from those early days of strife and parochial feuding.

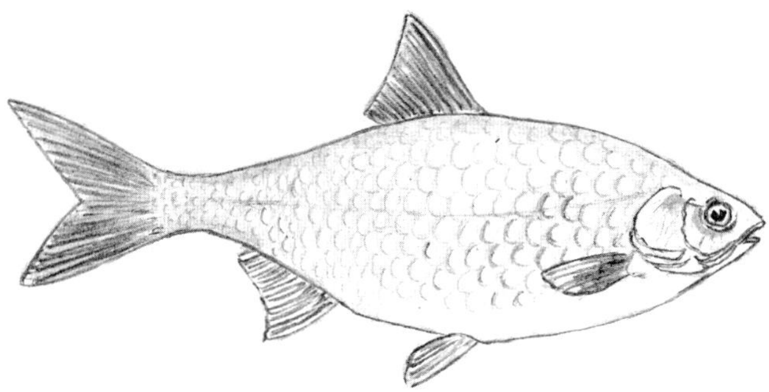

THE ASBESTOS SHOPS

Within the short space of time which witnessed the writing of my last collection of stories there has been additional change. Dunk's Corner has been further transported into a world of impersonal technology. Two sets of traffic lights, filter lanes, directional signs and a maze of road markings now confront the traffic.

So profound have been the changes that I am ever now confused as to exactly where the old Railway Inn stood. The public bar was probably suspended, so far as I can judge, above the present slip-lane from Hawkwell to Nailbridge for the quarry face which once prescribed the limit of the rear of the property is now hard-by the road. What does it matter!? Ghosts have no thirst! Not a vestige remains of the hedge to Dick Phillips's pike-house cottage. Alice Jordan's shop window is now a blank face of cement render and if you had stood there as in the past, contemplating the ha'penny goodies, you would have been quickly picked off by the passing traffic! Harper's cottage - well, where was it ever!? The quarry face glowers over a scene, of constant movement.

But the asbestos shops are still there.

They stand, well-back, on the left-hand side of the Mitcheldean to Monmouth lane, in the crotch between the main road and the acute branch road to Cinderford.

"The asbestos shops" is the unbeautiful name we, as children, gave them - because they were totally built of whitish, asbestos-cement sheets. They constituted a rectangular, single-storey building divided into three sections. At opposing ends were two shops, each with plate-glass windows, and their own recessed entrance porches. The middle section was a common warehouse. The whole stood upon a concrete platform giving it a somewhat grand elevation.

This design was the brain-child of my Uncle Fred Hale, son of blacksmith John Hale and founder of Hale & Co. It was meant as a retail outlet, the alternative premises at Nailbridge at that time being little more than a timber yard. The asbestos shops must have been built approximately when I was born because they have a permanent presence in my memory. In the space beside them was a single petrol pump but during my active boyhood at least, I never saw this pump used.

In 1938 my family took on the lease of the nearby bungalow which automatically included the lease of the asbestos shops. By this time they were used only for storing lumber.

From behind the door came a crescendo of exclamations and groans which brought on another attack of squirts. The thought that we had achieved a squirt of hairspray free was of great and childish triumph.

My parents first sublet the end shop nearest to the bungalow, to a barber. John Brain came from Drybrook and, for reasons which are obscure, possessed the unusual nickname of "Dig-dig." It may have had something to do with the popular jive-tune of the time, "A dig-dig-dig, well alright," but if it did, I never comprehended, accepting it without question, the way you do when you are young.

John Brain was not a particularly jivey character but he was alright! He cut our hair at reduced charges during the quiet times of his trade - which were frequent! We plagued him with pranks. One of the best was to creep into the common warehouse and then by whispering and causing mysterious scratching noises give the impression that we were spying through the keyhole of the locked common door. John in turn stealthily took his hair-spray which was operated by a rubber bulb, a standard piece of equipment in all barber shops, quickly inserted the nozzle into the keyhole and let go a mighty series of quirts! By this time, the one chosen by lot, was waiting, head down against the keyhole. From behind the door came a crescendo of exclamations and groans which brought on another attack of squirts and the second chosen got his! The thought that we had achieved a squirt of hair-spray free was of great and childish triumph.

These were the times of short hair styles. They say that in the Crimean War there was so much disease and pestilence the British Army ordered hair to be cropped to keep the lice at bay. This set a social fashion for over seventy years until, in fact, after the Second War. The style took on the hallmark of good, utilitarian manliness. Long hair was for women and cissies. A male with hair longer than about an inch and a half below his ears would have been derided to the point of ridicule.

"Wha's think a thick 'un? Fancy 'im's Lloyd Gearge, don' a?!"

(Prime Minister Lloyd George had long, greying locks well below his collar - in keeping with his reputation as a womaniser. This parody, together with the skeletal thinness of Mahatma Gandhi, the nationalistic scourge of the British in India, were in general household use in the thirties.)

Frequent visits to the barber's were socially essential to avoid ridicule from your school teachers and your school mates. Those who couldn't afford it got the pudding basin or the front-tuft clip. The pudding basin employed the services of a pudding basin, or several of them if necessary, and the cutting of every hair which protruded beyond the rim. The front-tuft clip took every hair down to the scalp except for a small bunch on the fringe. It took no skill! This tuft was a useful appendage to be seized by exasperated school teachers! It was also where the headlice dashed for cover and in which the school's inspection officer searched for them.

… two great hands wrapped about the skull, the scalp was assaulted in the most violent fashion until your ears rang.

Oh yes! Hair - or at least the lack of it - was an important part of a comfortable life.

Visits to the barber was by necessity on a Saturday morning. At such time the barber shops were crowded to overflowing. Youngsters mingled with old men wanting a shave. As many as three barbers slaved in front of the sinks and mirrors. The click of scissors played a constant tune.

Adults got measured and dignified respect - youngsters got roughed-up! Well, that's what it felt like! The scissors flew, a hand roughly jolted the head into position - the harder if the angle wasn't quite right! The hand-clippers gouged remorseless tracks from shoulders to a plimsoll line above the ears. There was no recourse. The dressing was standard Brylcream and you needed to shout quickly if you wanted the alternative, slightly cissy spray - otherwise you got the treatment - a squirt in the barber's palm of the cream - a quick slapping together of the hands and then the laying-on! Laying-on?! The two great hands wrapped about the skull, the scalp was assaulted in the most violent fashion until your ears rang. The comb descended and scratched the hair into parallel tracks divided by a straight parting from crown to fringe - for a boy, on the left, for a girl on the right. The sheet was ripped vigorously from the collar and what felt like a painter's dusting brush whacked about your neck for a few strokes. The feeling was memorable - cold, taut and immeasurably prickly. Your neck and shoulders itched for hours.

The coin pressed into the barber's palm was scarcely noticed. He was already shaking the sheet and looking for the follow-on.

"Next! Come on o'but. Don't waste all day!"

I always felt there was a curious connection between the words barber and barbarous! This was the ordeal of the barber's shop. Dig-dig's shop did away with all that pain. We were honoured clients.

Sadly, Dig-dig went away to war and died in the Western Desert under Rommel's guns. He achieved immortality in our minds though and even today I think of him and the clammy fragrance of the stolen hairspray.

After Dig-dig Brain came the Jehovah's Witnesses. They were stuck for a Kingdom Hall in the district and my mother, ever sympathetic with their movement's unflinching stance against Hitler's pogroms, leased them the warehouse part of the shops. For several years they held their services at Dunk's in the gloomy confines of the warehouse enlightened only by their shining posters.

Jehovah's Witnesses are pacifists. In the war this term was modified to "conchies", standing for conscientious objectors. They refused to do military service and many were directed onto the land as a result.

The presence of Kingdom Hall in my parents' shops was to me, a schoolboy, something of an embarrassment. I was constantly being accused of being a conchie and going to Watchtower meetings. The Watchtower was the journal of the Jehovah's Witnesses; it prescribed the elements for a faultless life. The missionary technique of the movement in those days, was, as today, doorstep calls. The best technology of the day was incorporated. Each carried a wind-up portable gramophone upon which the messages of the founder, the American, Judge Rutherford, were relayed. It was, I thought, quite unique. This technique has now been replaced by face to face debate. When they call at my door today, I remember the special relationship I had when the faithful were at Dunk's.

The Jehovah's Witnesses now have a very elegant modern church at Parkend - a far cry from the old asbestos shops.

I called at the shops the other day. They now house a firm of conservatory specialists. In the section where I had long, long ago sat in Dig-dig Brain's barber's chair there were two people, a man and a woman, busily working away at the details of some double-glazing projects. No, they were much to busy to talk about past times, but they were polite.

The door through which the hairspray came was sealed over. The ghost of Dig-dig was far away.

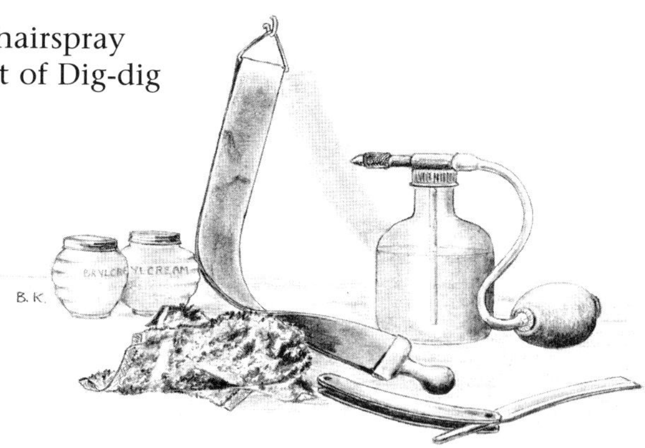

THE WAR YEARS

It so happened that the six-year incident of the Second World War - I call it an incident since although it had profound effects on the Forest these were not so much of a front-line order carrying the terror, say, of the London Blitz or the epic drama of the Battle of Britain over Kent - coincided with the years of my puberty and ended with my being called-up. 1939 to 1945 were years therefore of double-significance. They marked the passing of the old Forest to the new, the child to the semblance at least of an adult.

But this isn't an auto-biography. I am merely the agent passing on bits and pieces, diary-fashion and with a twist of humour. This period by consequence appears as through the eyes of a youth. It contains a before and after the War effect simply because it was happening that way both personally and nationally. Some of the accounts are merely contemporary with the War years and not directly a part of or a result of the conflict. Others could have happened at no other time.

One feature of wartime was the lack of published news owing of course, to national security. Local news from that period is just not available. Accounts from the horses' mouths, so to speak, are the more valuable

Before the war, in the Forest, there was a degraded and impoverished industrial scene in which a proud and hard-working population languished. The fact that it was more of a true forest than it had been for centuries - ie. unbroken stretches of mature trees, mainly oak - and the presence of unattended relics of industrial enterprise in the form of open mine shafts, crumbling buildings, derelict ponds and spoil heaps - made it an adventure playground par excellence - but not without grave dangers to boot.

The following text is not therefore a single story but a series of incidents drawn from the spectrum of the war years and just before, a kaleidoscope of images against which I can put no exact dates but all of which fall in this critical period.

The Forest used to be one of the country's main producers of iron. In order to smelt iron you need lime and in order to produce lime you need limestone and a furnace. The process was crude. You required an airtight chamber and

The disused lime kilns were much beloved of Forest sheep who crowded into them littering the floor with a cake of dry and semi-dry sheep's muck. They would scramble up with that curious horny rattling of the dry clods of dung hanging in what we called clumpers from their coats.

a slow, continuous heat. The Forest was peppered with these lime kilns. They were brick-lined chambers built into the ground, an arched, oven-shaped opening in the front. In disuse they provided useful shelter for sheep and even for homeless human beings.

I never saw one working in producing lime, though they were very much a part of the 1930s scene. In hot weather they were much beloved of Forest sheep who crowded into them littering the floor with a cake of dry and semi-dry sheep's muck. The high odour of sheep dung and the clouds of bluebottles made these kilns out-of-bounds in summer. But we achieved some fun in stampeding the animals out of them. The sheep seemed to recognise that they had no alternative means of egress other than the kiln's entrance and if you shouted *"Giddup!"* to the closely-packed, twitching mob, they would scramble up with that curious, horny, rattling sound peculiar only to sheep and caused partly by their hooves and partly by the rattling of the dry clods of dung hanging from their coats! They would then charge out in a jockeying throng through the narrow tunnel entrance and we would whoop them off through the woods with a great sense of achievement!

My parents forbade me to enter these disused kilns, because, they warned, they might contain carbon dioxide. Apparently, in the old days, paupers desperate for the warmth imparted by the hot limestone and a shelter over their heads, had crept into a lime kiln, fallen asleep and never wakened.

In the main I obeyed. But there were other, even greater hazards in that litter of industrial remains. Some of these I have described in an earlier account and I hesitate therefore, to drag my readers through all these sometimes amusing but dangerous pranks.

One thing we had before the war, was a dedicated medical service. Let no-one complain that this service suffered the bad morale and the over-work which afflicts our modern NHS. The service might have been deficient - medical knowledge short, equipment primitive and many debilities inherent - but the doctors visited you in your home! I say again lest you do not hear me - the doctors had a daily round and, without question and as a matter of course - visited you in your home! They might have been autocratic and at times over-bearing but they came.

Together with the headmaster, the solicitor and the vicar, doctors formed the Establishment in the district.

Our family doctor was Old Sumption. He wasn't particularly old - perhaps in his fifties - but my mother called him that as did many others on his panel. It was more a name of endearment than of disrespect.

He would conduct his morning surgery from the cold, unheated and dank waiting room in Drybrook. After the last patient, he took to his rounds rather grandly, in a Daimler or some such antique motor. He arrived at the homes of his patients some time between mid-morning and lunch - later if busy. Hot water and a clean towel had to be on hand as a matter of course and I can see him now, his hands flapping in a rather helpless pose after an examination, demanding peevishly, *"Hot water."* He literally breezed in and out of your house radiating faint odours of medicinal origin.

He was a large man with fat, white, sensitive hands and short stubby fingers with which he was able to thump your chest eliciting a most interesting resonance - a thing I tried to achieve in my own privacy but never with success. His stethoscope was diagnostic - that cold, magical disc which he laid carefully at different points accompanied by a sort of chant, *"Breathe in ... Breathe out ... Breathe in ... Breathe out,"* changing the position of the disc with every command.

Invariably, the treatment was medicine - not pills. Charlie Bower, the local chemist, dispensed this by mixing the actual ingredients in a standardly recognisable, clear glass bottle about six inches tall closed with a cork stopper. The bottle carried a label which gave the dosage and always the inscription, *"Shake Well"*. This was backed up by the nature of the liquid inside which varied from mud colour to clear and contained an inch or so of suspended powder which sank quickly accumulating thickly in the bottom. A vigorous shake put the whole lot once more into suspension. The taste was always appalling - bitter with various undertones of unfamiliar unpleasantness! Occasionally - just occasionally - as with some of the cough cures, the flavour was sweet and aromatic - bearing liquorish or the same flavours you got in tiny chloro gums, pear drops, menthol drops or peppermints. This was a great relief.

Old Sumption was invariably sarcastic. My mother always put on a snorting fit after he had departed labelling him with many unkind epithets.

When I became a youth I developed painful and disfiguring acne. Packets of fatty, unmentionable material under my skin turned to suppurating lumps. In desperation, I betook myself to Doctor Sumption's surgery.

With a sigh of irritation I thought, he set down the pencil he normally kept in his fingers ready to write out the inevitable prescription. He eyed me up and down, not bothering even to look at that particularly large swollen pimple I had on the back of my neck and had been the last straw promoting the visit. With great disdain he coughed and with a sort of hoarse, refined voice I knew so well, said, *"You are - you must remember, Mr Christian - just a hobble-de-hoy. Yours is a condition of all hobble-de-hoys and if you are patient, it will pass - next month, next year or, if you are unlucky, in five or six years' time!"*

I left the surgery hopeless and chastened. *"Bloody Old Sumption!"*

The Thirties seemed set to continue indefinitely, unchangingly, the signs of extreme poverty and harsh working conditions going hand in hand with poor health.

Then on the 3rd September 1939, Prime Minister Chamberlain announced that if Germany did not call off its invasion of Poland by eleven o'clock, Britain and Germany would be in a state of war. I remember my parents saying the RAF were dropping upon Berlin leaflets urging peace and that perhaps the Germans would stop. Some bloody chance and everyone knew it! By eleven o'clock we were at war.

It took time but the old regime in the Forest had gone. Unemployment was a past conception and coal a dire necessity for the War Effort. A collier was expected to shift about fifteen tons of coal a day. But it was not until 1943 that the Ministry of Labour under Ernie Bevin used its emergency powers to direct part of the conscripted manpower into the pits. One in ten conscripts were compulsorily directed into the mines. They were called Bevin Boys. Bevin was an ex Union leader coopted into the wartime cabinet and an extremely tough and powerful character.

The Bevin Boys themselves bitterly resented the order and considered the mines as a poor alternative to the glamour of the Forces. But the process opened up the public consciousness as to the awful privations of the miners. Ironically too, it all demoinstrated the poor deal the miners had been receiving. It was found for instances that women munition workers were being paid as much as three times the amount of a coal face miner! The Bevin Boy scheme was probably one of the most potent forces in remodelling the mining industry when the war finished.

Though the writing was on the wall for the mining industry, for the time being the demand for coal superceded the restraints of poor economy, profit and loss and the coal mining industry in the Forest got a kick in the pants.

New people came into the Forest for no other reason than to get away from dangerous areas. Some were even refugees from Europe. Others were evacuees from British industrial cities. My schooling was quickly modified by the evacuation of a complete school from Birmingham to the school premises for each second half of the day. Some days, barring sport, we could catch the bus to Five Acres, walk to Mirey Stock and catch Lardy Kear's miners' bus taking the early shift from Waterloo Screens! It was a scamper and I recall hurrying down the seemingly endless Long Hill hoping the shift had been delayed. The basic old Ford truck with the door in the back to which a steep set of steps rose would grind to a halt at the end of the pit road when the driver saw the gaggle of breathless schoolboys waiting. We would clamber up the steps aided by strong, blackened hands that came out of the darkness,

"Come on in my butty! Come on an' sit over 'ere by I. Watch thee clothes mind. I don't want thee fayther a'ter I fer a contribution to thee new suit!"

It was all well-meant despite the gritty laughter all round

The greeting made us swell with pride - being pulled in to that grimy, dust encrusted interior which smelled of rank tobacco and pit clay and rough clothes. The miners would sit there on the hard, wooden seats and grin at us their white teeth flashing in the blackened faces.
By golly! - that was living!

The war did not put any constraints on the youth of the district. It added to the scope. We were already in that unsatisfiable state that causes a hiatus in in the progress of all things - adolescence - the pause before the opening

We would climb up the steps aided by the strong, blackened hands that came out of the darkness.

up of the whole world - or at least the bit we comprehended from the newspapers and the wireless.

By 1940 we were gathering in the lobbies of the asbestos shops after evenings of harrying Dig-dig Brain. Nevertheless, we were always on the lookout for some new adventure.

My Uncle Bland Greening was the hairiest man I ever knew. The most remarkable thing about him however, was that he was already prematurely bald. His head had developed a fine, shiny pate surrounded by a neat tonsure of jet black hair - while from his cuffs and shirt front projected great strands of black, coarse hair like the contents of a broken-down chaise-longue! He was a figure commanding some considerable degree of respect.

He was also sergeant of the local Home Guard unit. Composed of quite young, fit miners and other reserved trades; this Home Guard had no resemblance to the aged and fairly ineffective Dad's Army!

One October as the autumn nights drew in, my pal and I discovered my father's bucket of potato rejects he was saving to boil up for the fowls. Excellent missiles, we armed ourselves with pocketfuls and waited for the Home Guard nightly patrol along the road below the quarry. As they passed our ambush we let them have volley after volley of small potato missiles from the darkening trees above the rockface.

Repeated exclamations and expletives gave audible proof we were scoring hits.

The patrol quickly identified the source of the attack and stormed the high-point. We retreated at speed through the wood. The HG followed in open skirmishing order bayonets fixed and safety catches off - or at least that's what they said afterwards.

If it wasn't for my pal I would have evaded capture. Concealed in long bracken the Home Guard would have passed through us. At the last moment he up and broke through the advancing line. They were ready for me though. I ran into the strong arms of a burly collier.

"My boy - we might've shot you! We thought you were escaped German prisioners!" (Why would escaped prisoners attack with small potatoes?!)

But it was enough to put me into severe shock!
I think the Home Guard enjoyed the fun.

The war effort demanded labour. Anyone and everyone was expected to be employed. And so we, as schoolboys could get temporary work with the Crown in the local woods, planting, ditching, carrying-out (felled timber), weeding , brush-burning - a number of non-skilled jobs.

This employment provided us with a meagre income. We were the first of the spending teenagers - a market which, after the war, was to grow into something quite economically significant. Ten bob a week after all, was something akin to £50 a week in current terms!

There wasn't too much to spend one's money on in wartime especially. One of the leading sources of evening entertainment was *The Palace*. Needless to say The Palace was not a palace nor yet a nightclub; such had not come to our social scene! The Palace was a cinema. Here, two main films and two subsidiary films were shown every week changing Monday to Wednesday and Thursday to Saturday. There was no performance on Sundays.

It is difficult to stress how important was this source of entertainment to the populace. Many attended - yes, that's the word, attended - twice a week; whatever the film. We watched some awful films! - in particular the 'B' films which preceeded the main feature film, changing after a string of adverts when the lights went up and ice creams were sold. (Ice cream production never ceased during the war.)

The Palace was an old music hall theatre. It was typical. A narrow entrance foyer housed the ticket office staffed by Miss Jones. One proceeded inside either to the stalls or the balcony, up the stairs. The stalls had two sections - the neckbreakers in the front rows and the rear stalls. The balcony too had two sections - the circle (front) and the circle (back). The rowdies went in the neckbreakers, often moving back by climbing over the seats when the lights dimmed. The refined elements went to the balcony.

A surge of people running down to The Swan would swarm onto the bus.

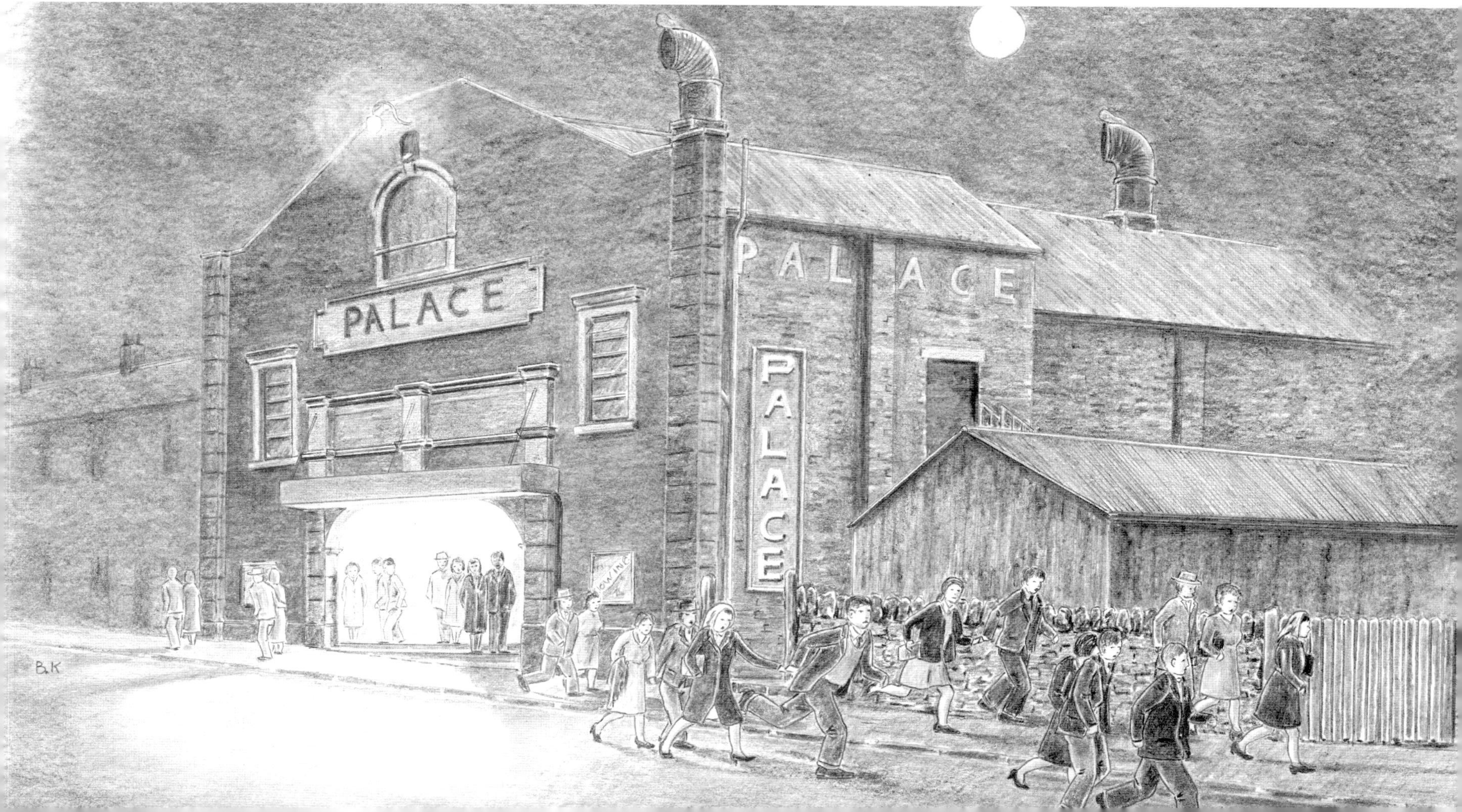

Smoking was permitted and almost endemic. When you looked up during the screening, the projection beams cut dramatic, thinly tapered channels through a dense screen of tobacco smoke; the lighting of each new fag sent a swirl of new, blue smoke surging through these. Every seat had a little brass tray screwed to its back for cigarette ash which however became packed with screwed -up ice cream wrappers, sweet papers and apple cores.

If you took your girlfriend you took the back rows. In the balcony of The Palace there was a sort of superstructure of match-boarding around the entrance stairs which tapered away to two pairs of double seats immediately at the back. These were excellent for snogging - then called necking - which went on very discreetly.

When the main film ended and the curtain swung down the National Anthem was played. The polite and patriotic remained sedate, standing reverently at the first chords of the great tune and remaining thus until the last chords died away. The undedicated broke loose before the titles had finished and were scurrying for the exit before the NA came on, elbowing, shoving, behaving like a lot of n'ere do wells!

Often this rush was justified; they wanted to catch the last bus. If you lived out of town you had to make it or walk home. A surge of people running down to The Swan would swarm onto the bus - often as it moved out. Obliging drivers would ease up. Others would accelerate and leaping people would cling to the entrance rail to haul themselves aboard.

(The Palace Cinema was refurbished and re-opened as a cinema in March 2001).

Films were an important adjunct to wartime morale. America, at first not in the war, continued to make films which, because of the special relationship, were imported. Our own films made at Ealing and Denholme, were strongly propagandist in content. John Mills, Noel Coward, Bill Owen, Jack Hawkins, Bernard Miles, Anna Neagle and many others collaborated on celluloid to strengthening the British stiff upper lip.

On the ground in the Forest, the war proceeded distantly. If you stood on the southwest ridges during the air raids you could see Bristol getting it. A glow lit up the sky there and within it, minute pinpricks of light between the sweeping rays of the searchlights showed the anti-aircraft shells bursting. If you watched long enough you might see a very bright object light up suddenley in one of the beams and be held there for a few seconds; an enemy plane caught knapping but as often as not lost again into the obscurity of the night. Flashes of light marked the sticks of bombs as they fell but little sound reached our ears.

Sometimes an enemy bomber would stray wide of the theatre of action and come droning north over the Forest. The sound of a German bomber could always be distinguished from a British plane they said, because it had a peculiar throbbing note - *"Growl - owl - owl - owl - owl......"* The fact was no other British planes were likely to be aloft during a raid except fighters which had a totally different light-weight sound.

In the main, these stray bombers had voided their bomb-load and were dispersing from the target zone prior to heading home. Occasionally one was looking for a soft target out of the hot operations zone. A stray light or sign of activity on the ground would cause the bomber to release his bombs and go home.

Generally then, the Forest received few bombs. One was when an enemy bomber saw the glow of the brick kilns at Hawkwell. He may have thought this was a raid fire so he let go his stick roughly in a north to south direction. The bombs fell from Ruardean Hill to Nofold Green killing a pony I believe.

I remember the sound of that bomber and the scream of the stick coming down followed by the crump of bursts. But by that time I was heading full tilt for the air-raid shelter my father had built in the garden but which had rarely, if ever been used!

In the morning my pal and I were first out on our bikes to find the still smoking craters with their rims of churned earth. We searched the chaos for shrapnel. A nose-cone or a bit of casing with lettering still on it was a prize indeed. The crater where one of those bombs landed just behind Cartwright's

Beneath the trees were stored many tons of high explosives and, in one area, mustard gas.

house outside Newtown was there for many, many years, eventually filled with briars and weeds and unrecognisable as a bomb site. It has now been obliterated as part of the general development in that area,

It was as well the Forest had no serious air raids. Beneath the trees were stored many tons of high explosive and, in one area, mustard gas. This was in the form of shells - minus their detonators but potentially lethal just the same. They appeared in stacks beside the roads eventually to be covered by open-ended, semi-circular corrugated iron shelters. They were completely open to access and possible disturbance, say, in the same way many public structures are now attacked by vandals! Perhaps vandals - such as they existed in those days - had got the message that these things were dangerous. Anyway, the shells stayed there throughout the best part of the war without interference but without any edict to protect them. The Forest was eventually a vast arsenal protected only by the tree cover. At Drybrook the disused Bailey Tunnel was stuffed with high explosive belonging to the Navy the detonation of which would have sent Drybrook to Kingdom Come.

We took all this very much for granted and unquestioningly. The shells appeared of course without any official announcement. It was very much a case of thinking they looked dangerous and one having had seen pictures of similar objects going into the breeches of guns. But the certainty was speculative and so no-one got too excited about it.

There was however, some concern. The Germans presumably never learnt of the arsenal for there was never any clear attack on the Forest. At the same time their radio propaganda was working hard to demoralize the population. Every evening Germany broadcast in English to the English people through a commentary by the traitorous announcer William Joyce, alias Lord Haw-Haw. His sardonic voice became well-known to radio listeners and one night, according to the story, he announced that the village clock at Newnham was five minutes slow! *(Humphrey Phelps's book The Forest of Dean in Wartime. Pub Alan Sutton 1945, says it was Blakeney clock.)* This alarmed many. The inference was if he knew the clock was slow he also knew of the piles of shells up in the Forest. If, by some clever process of espionage he knew the former, events show he certainly did not know the latter.

I have a letter from a resident, a girl during the war, who lived at Varnister Farm above Drybrook. She says her mother heard Lord Haw-Haw say on the radio that the Germans knew of the Naval shells at Drybrook and would soon be sending the village to oblivion. Her mother was greatly shocked and apprehensive which isn't surprising. Some strangers camping near the farm were branded as the spies who had passed on the information. The Germans never got Drybrook and the local ladies continued to go daily to dust and polish the shells to preserve them in good order.

The village clock at Newnham was five minutes slow!

The war progressed more or less from day to day in this fashion. The lives of the people were not greatly changed but there was less privation. The war did what socialism had failed to achieve, by rationing and allocation and by exhortation, it spread the resources more evenly; some received less, many received rations which were greater than their social status would have achieved beforehand. Prices were controlled except on the black market and in the countryside where everyone seemed to know everyone else, the operation was based on goodwill rather than profit.

Then one day in 1943 - the exact date is almost impossible to trace - the Yanks arrived.

Not Yankies, nor yet Doughboys as in the 1914/18 War, they were to the local inhabitants, plain Yanks - pronounced Yanx as if with an 'X'. The shock on the district was enormous. Here, after all, into one of the most conservative (with a small 'c'), the most insular, the most unchanging society you could hope to find in the British Isles, was injected a microcosm of the most advanced and affluent society the World, up to that date, had known.

Visitors had rarely come to the Forest of Dean; there was not much here to attract them except coal and so much timber you couldn't see the wood for the trees. The Yanks, in their true national form, were not exactly compatible with the average Britisher, let alone the average Forester! Class awareness, reserve, deprivation, female chastity - all were social qualities the Yanks knew nothing about. They came with their brashness, their promiscuity, their nylons, their chocolate and chewing gum and took over by sheer weight of numbers; a drawl and a touch of honey-babe; it did the trick!

There were strict codes of discipline to keep the twain apart but clearly you could not keep a modern army confined to barracks.

American Forces were positioned in several parts of the Dean. They were employed on a number of duties. The ones I recall best were those who came to the twenty or so acres of remote woodland just outside Drybrook in a forest inclosure at Mitcheldean Meend (of which more anon.) These arrived overnight as it were and theirs was to be a specific task; they were part of the holding force for the highly secret invasion of Europe.

Although the local pubs were out-of-bounds, the local dancehall was open house. Here, on a Saturday-night hop, was the interface!

The American Camp at the Stenders - at the Saturday hop Brewsters, Bilkos and Botewskis fought Boseleys, Brains and Baldwins

It wasn't as if the district was peopled by an ageing population too old for the battlefield. Here, in the coal mines and on the land, young, fit, virile men were required in reserved occupations. They objected to their girlfriends being taken over, dazzled by those chocolates, limitless cigarettes and, at the last seduction, nylon stockings. Younger brothers were won over by chewing gum and candy. Now I'm not suggesting Forest maids were disloyal - it was merely that they were good opportunists! But it didn't do any good for the stress psychology of the Forest boys.

There were battles, blows, harsh words. Boseleys, Brains and Baldwins fought Bilkos, Brewsters and Botewskis!

I'm not going to comment on the rights or wrongs of those battles. I and my friends were mere boys witnessing the needle, the trysts in the woods. We benefitted sometimes from receiving packs of strange, long slabs of chewing gum - quite unlike the stubby, uncool, white, sugar-coated lozenges of British gum - supplied by older sisters. We searched the woodland glades for the manifestations of fraternisation, becoming expert at hounding out the patches of flattened grass.

Later, I became the recipient of a splendid American Army combat tunic, a garment so superior to the coarse, serge equivalent of the British Army that I wore it for several years in the forestry and for many years after that. Neither rain, wind nor snow penetrated its formidable protection. It was of the finest, tightest cotton-gabardine with woven cotton collar and cuffs. Inside it was lined with serge. A deep, shielded zip closed it and the back was amply expandable by the provision of two deep pleats running each side from shoulder to waste.

This beautiful and stylish piece of clothing was left by its owner, hanging on a nail behind the back-kitchen door; its owner, rapidly transported to France, never returned for it.

A short time before D-day, June 6 1944, the Yanks up and left - literally over-night. No one of course knew they were going just as no one had anticipated their arrival. One day there were the huts, the smoking flue-pipes, the bustle of camp life, the next there was merely a pioneer battalion with giant bulldozers pushing it all into the ground. It was as eerie as that.

Mitcheldean Meend, wherein I would later spend a winter of my life working for the Crown, would return to its solitude.

Farther up on Wigpool Common proper, there is, I understand, the remnant of a sealed-off cave, one of the great fissures in the limestone rim of the Forest basin. This cave used to be known to local inhabitants as Jesus Weeping - or as my old friend Jim Hale called it by local dialect, "Jesus a-weeping", which somehow seems more expressive. I never got to see it but by all accounts the name arose from a column of white limestone, the base perhaps of some ancient stalagmite, which resembled the figure of Christ weeping over the sins of Man. This cave, again by all accounts, was vast enough to house the camp cinema. It is a unique and dramatic story to imagine all those American soldiers watching some Hollywood film in the bowels of the earth, beneath the tearful eyes of Christ. Here, they were invisible from the prying eyes of spies and saboteurs.

When the soldiers left, this cave was packed with redundant stores and sealed off with concrete. In my youth, as an avid follower of the American swing bands of the era, I was told of invaluable piles of American V-discs - the 12 inch gramophone records especially produced for entertainment of the American forces and much prized by we worshippers of Count Basie, Glen Miller and the like - heaped in there and reduced perhaps to shards of crushed shellac. But maybe many survived?! It was my dream that someday the concrete would be broken by a latter-day archaeologists to reveal a Tutankhamun hoard of recorded jazz! One day perhaps! One never knows!

The story of the Yanks at Drybrook might now as well be pure myth. You see, as a matter of national security it was not reported, not at the time, not as ongoing news. After D-Day there was still restriction and in any case other international events of huge magnitude eclipsed all the little local stories. The record remained only in the memories of those present. Many years after, I am reliably told, a researcher contacted the American Embassy library asking for the dates when the American Forces were stationed at Drybrook. The terse reply came that there was no record of American troops having ever been in Drybrook!

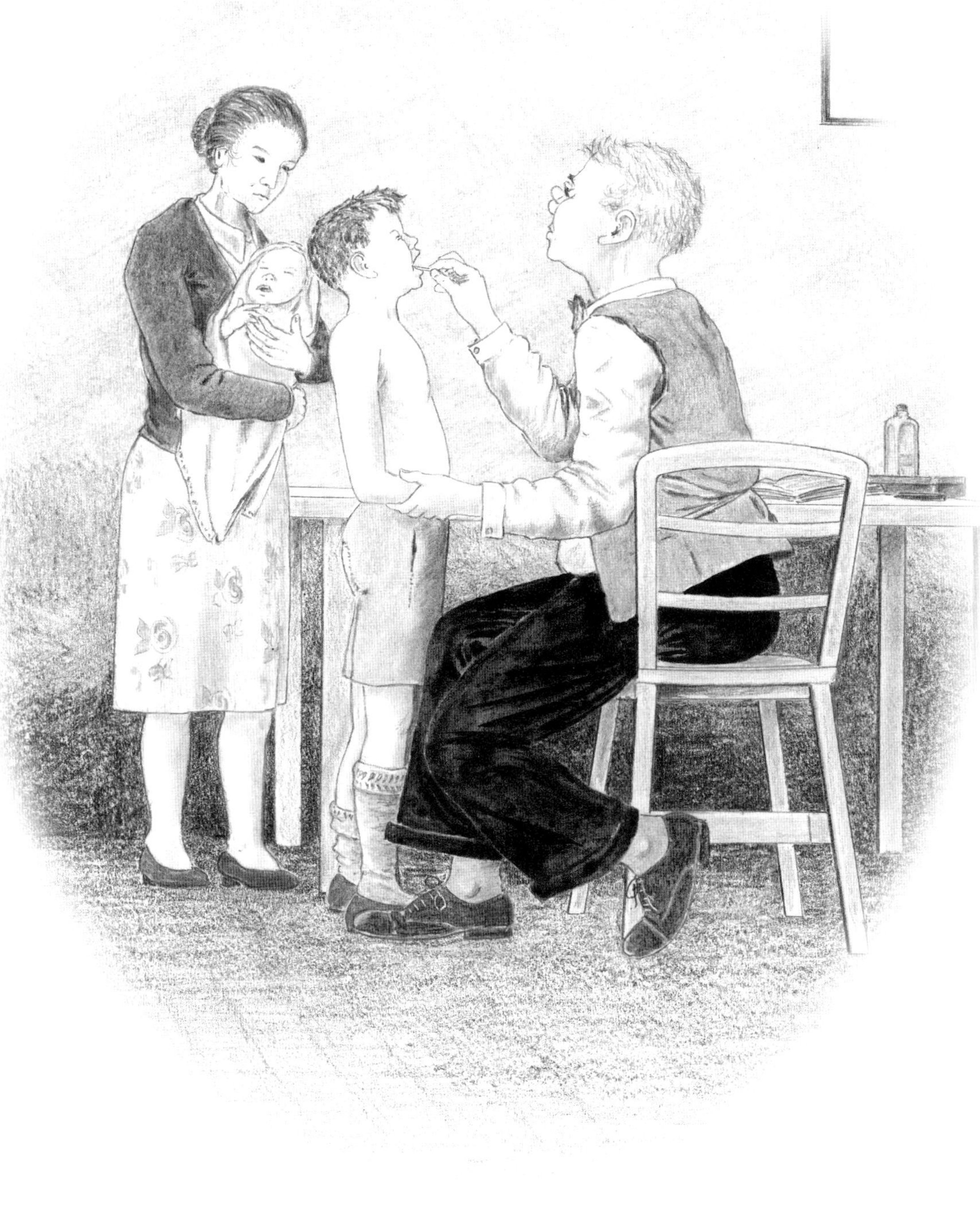

Scene from a pre-war surgery

THE BLACKOUT

The war may have been relatively a long way from the Forest but it affected the every-day activities of the residents as it did all over the Country in a number of apparently minor ways. Not least of these was the blackout.

It became a legal requirement of the extraordinary requisites of wartime that no naked or exposed light should be allowed to give the enemy guidance whether by plane or by any other presence. Wardens were appointed with powers to demand that exposed lights be immediately extinguished. The shout, *"Put that light out!"* became a catchphrase of the war; sometimes an expletive was added! Ordinary people going about their business used it apart from the wardens. It was almost a friendly greeting because everyone, from time to time, allowed the curtains to slip or the blackout sheet fell down or they kept the door open too long. We lived in a bible-black world, all of us, creeping, feeling our way round while the German planes droned overhead trying to seek us out.

Now the Forest prior to 1939 had never been a particularly well-lit place. We were all conditioned to the use of torches or lanterns in order to get from place to place after dark. So one might have construed that this was a mere hiccup in the course of our living. It was however, the sheer finality of the order that made things difficult. Not a chink of light was allowed.

Not much motorised traffic was at that time present on the roads but what there was had to be in pursuit of business of an essential nature. Doctors needed to get to emergency calls. Most workers were dependent upon public transport in order to reach their place of work. How could one drive along the poor roads without a guiding light of some sort?

The problem was met by the designing and fitting of headlamp shields which took the form of blanking plates inserted over the face of the headlamp. Into this shield was cut a narrow slot in turn shielded from above by a little eyebrow of metal. The result was a meagre glow of light, just enough to allow a vehicle to creep along the road. Remember, cats' eyes had not been invented; the verges were black voids. Just how profound this lightless situation was is difficult to describe. Suffice it to say that one night when I missed the last bus connection from Coleford, I had to walk from Broadwell to Cinderford past the Speech House. Had it not been for the ring of my boots on tarmac I wouldn't have known if I was on the right route!

So, we crept about our business after dark like crepuscular creatures, feeling rather than seeing our way about. Life after dark was largely confined to activity within the four walls of one's home where the blackout curtains were an absolute barrier between you and the night outside.

And so it was that on the blackest night of Friday, March 15th 1940 old Absy Phelps was making his way home towards Steam Mills and its neighbouring hamlet of Newtown where he lived by courtesy of the Morgan family, in a modest timber hut at the bottom of their garden.

According to my old friend Hedley Morgan then a small boy in his family's home, *"Twas a tidy hut"*. It gave Absy the independence his character wanted.

I have tried, but failed, to find out anything more about the old man. He was at the time, a well-known local eccentric but no member of his family has come forward in response to my requests. His background is totally obscure. Whether he had been a miner or a forestry worker or whatever remains a mystery.

The name Absy, sometimes pronounced Apsy, was presumably short for Absalom. Phelps is a fequently occurring family name from the district.

The Forest was peopled by a number of characters renowned in the community for their eccentricity in those days. Today we might say that they had fallen through the net of social care. But they were totally unlike the pitiable social wrecks which are presently found mainly in urban environs. Many were quite capable of sustaining themselves - survival experts living under circumstances which you or I might eschew. The vastness of the woods absorbed them and eased the squalor of their lives. Some lived in old lime-kilns, some in derelict buildings or in remote cottages which gave them solitude and which no other person had designs upon. Some bore the terrible afflictions resulting from the First War.

I remember Absy as a lumbering old man dressed in a variety of derelict garb but always wearing a tall and battered felt hat pushed to the back of his head in hot weather but never discarded. He carried a walking stick which again I recall as the long, thumbstick variey. His boots - often the measure of a man's poverty - were solid and robust. He struck one as being of the country rather than of the mines - a stockman, a horse doctor, a hustler. I never recall him as a beggar; I may be wrong.

Anyway, on that Friday night - the blackest of nights - he had enjoyed his usual, Friday-night four pints of cider at the Railway Inn at Dunk's Corner. Ted Hughes the landlord said he had never seen the old man under the influence of drink. Dr Sumption said that for his age of seventy the old man was not unhealthy at all.

As he was pursuing his way home from the inn just after 10 pm, Bonser's colliers' bus was setting out from the opposite direction in Cinderford carrying the night shift probably to Northern United Pit or to Cannop or Waterloo. Horace Bonser was driving as he had done for very many years in the family business. The bus picked up a few men in Steam Mills then proceeded on in the direction of Hawkwell.

When Absy reached Steam Mills School a man who knew him - and most knew him - was waiting on the side of the road, possible for the colliers' bus itself. Anyway, he called out to Absy, who - as was his wont like hundreds of other Foresters - was walking in the centre of the road, *"Thee's wanna watch theeself mind, a-walkin' down the middle o' th'road like that. Get theeself run over!"*

It was said more in jest than in seriousness - a sort of standard quirky type of Forest greeting with one eyebrow raised. Absy might have responded, *"Oy! Thee's want!"*or words to that effect. He proceeded on towards Newtown without deviation.

About half-way between the school and the village the bus came rattling along perhaps at a steady 25 mph. Horace Bonser, giving evidence after, said all of a sudden a face appeared between the dimmed headlights and disappeared as soon as it had appeared. It took the bus a few yards to stop. The miners ran back and found Absy sprawled in the road, his old hat in one place and his stick in another. He was dead.

The great enigma, never explained, was that though coming from opposite directions neither Horace Bonser or Absy saw the other until the fatal impact. It was not even a bad night. It is perhaps pertinent to mention that in the stretch of road between the school and Steam Mills there used to be a sudden hump-back bridge under which the horse-drawn tramline running from Bowson to Nailbridge passed. This was dismantled and levelled just

The two met fatally in the lea of the bridge outside Steam Mills.

after the war and you would not now know it ever existed. But there it was, this little, humpty structure, so vertical that riding your bicycle at speed could produce a dramatic lift. It was certainly high enough to obscure the miner's bus from Absy and Absy from the driver and I suspect this is where the explanation lay. The two met fatally in the lea of this bridge.

Horace Bonser they say, never got over the shock though he was exonerated of all blame. Absy assumed the name of one of those minor casualties of the war scarcely noticed in all the greater carnage and misery.

Absy Phelps was not the only innocent victim of wartime. There are undoubtedly those who still mourn over the tragic incident of Ron Smith.

Ron Smith was a much respected resident of Drybrook who ran the bakery there. He was one of the fifty, nationwide, accidentally killed by the Home Guard during its early chaotic days.

His story dates from the early part of the war when the country was struggling to come to terms with the possibilities of a German invasion. The Home Guard or as it was first called, the LDV, was in its infancy, unfamiliar perhaps with the more subtle codes of discipline.

The date was the 23rd of August 1940 and in that stress of suspecting that spies abounded everywhere there were patrols along most of the roads with orders to check the dimly lit vehicles which passed them from time to time.

Ron Smith was a special constable. Together with his fellow constable, W G Robbins, the headmaster of Ruardean School, he was driving home having been on duty in the area. At the road junction near the Bailey Inn at Yorkley, a patrol of three Home Guard equipped only with a small hand-torch "the size of a packet of twenty cigarettes" were checking vehicles. They were armed with one loaded rifle between them and had orders to stop all vehicles. If a vehicle failed to stop they were empowered to shoot under their emergency orders.

This combination of poor equipment together with an element of unlucky coincidence was to lead to the death of Ron Smith. The patrol signalled with the tiny torch for the car to stop. Undoubtedly the driver failed to see the signal and drove on. One of the Home Guard fired at the disappearing car perhaps at the tyres, the bullet was deflected off the chassis through the interior seats into Ron Smith's body. The car swerved off the road. He was taken into the Bailey Inn where Dr Tandy pronounced life to have expired. The Forest was plunged into grief at the unnecessary death of this highly respected man. The Home Guard, as with all the other 49 tragic cases across the Country, were exonerated from blame.

On 30th April 1945 Adolph Hitler put a bullet through his head and the war was over shortly after.

Most of the people who had come to the Forest for reasons other than desire, left and returned to their native parts. Some remained having set up a love affair with the place and perhaps with one or other of its inhabitants. The importance of coal in the national budget would rapidly decline and those wet old pits of the Forest with their pitched and shattered seams would quickly close - Cannop, Eastern United, Norchard, Northern United and Princess Royal would all go in quick succession and their names become assigned to the past. The colliers, apprehensive about their futures and that of their offspring, would nevertheless become employed in better paid and more healthy occupations making biscuits, making copying machines, making fruit drinks. The newly planted woods would grow steadily, the fast conifers cut and the whole remodelled. The hand-labour and its good old tools - axes, cross-cut saws, dibbers, bill hooks and the like - would be replaced by mechanisation.

A fresh wind blew through the trees.

Acknowledgements to the Forest of Dean Newspapers and to Humphrey Phelps's The Forest in Wartime. Pub Alan Sutton.

THE CROWN

PINGARY'S PATCH

I seem to have spent my life pondering the origins of the term *meend*, a word which is peculiarly local to the Forest of Dean. It occurs as the place-name to a number of locations - Coleford Meend, Eastbach Meend, Merring Meend, Mitcheldean Meend, Drybrook Meend, the Meend Gardens, Cinderford and probably others which are not represented on any map but borne in the local awareness that passes from mouth to mouth.

A H Smith informs us in his *English Place-names of Gloucestershire* that the terms meend and mesne are from the same root meaning a wasteland. I must confess I understood the two had totally different origins. I had the idea that meend meant high ground above a particular village or town.

Now there is no reason why the high ground above a community should not be a wasteland, bleak, barren, thin of soil, unproductive, a receptical for the communty's waste. The only thing against this is that there are few locations in the Forest where such barrenness might occur - not, for instance, as on the top of a Welsh mountain.

A second reason is that system of land tenure in the Dean has been totally different to, say, that of the feudal lowlands. Land has been mostly owned by the Crown; commoners' rights have been frequent and definitive. There were few people in the Forest and the idea of a communal wasteland attached to each community is not realistic.

Clifford's Mesne near Newent is not on high ground and has no characteristic common with the high meends of Dean. I am convinced therefore that mesne does not have the same root as the true Forest *meends*. These are, with few exceptions, deep in Crown land, not commons in any sense and certainly, during recent years, mostly woodland.

A Gaelic word for a young roe deer is *meann* and one wonders perhaps, in the years when the Dean was a royal hunting forest, these were not places where roe deer were raised or likely to be raised. It is a nice thought but in this case, probably not so.

The true answer jumped out at me from the pages of Nicholls's *Iron Making in the Forest of Dean.*

The word is of course, of Celtic origin. There is a word in Welsh, mwyn or mwn meaning ore or mineral. Nicholls, describing the ancient digging of iron ore says, *"of these deeper workings, one of the most extensive occurs in the Lining Wood Hill above Mitcheldean ... They are met with on both sides of the Forest - in fact wherever the ore crops out, giving the name 'meand' to such places."*

Here it was, as clear as the nose on your face and obviously correct because all the meends mapped are manifestly associated with the digging of iron ore and display the presence of scowle holes and ancient, often prehistoric, workings.

I am prepared to seek no further, though I accept that such is the pedantry in the world of etymology that some may challenge.

Let it be said however, that the Forest meends are places of mystic origin, sacred perhaps, where the ghosts of the past linger, whispering their stories of pre-history.

My best, well-loved meend is that lying on the hill above Mitcheldean sharing with an adjacent area, Drybrook Meend - though I can find no mention of the latter on any map. Mitcheldean Meend is the more positively delineated.

It forms a wooded area, suspended as it were, on the rim of the steep rampart of rock which falls away to the town of Mitcheldean in the valley below. At its northern end it gives way to Wigpool. On its southern boundary it shares a border with Drybrook Meend, the two separated by a long, straight, unmade road running from the Stenders to the Deep Cutting.

Mitcheldean Meend is high, undulating around the 800 foot contour. In winter it is a cold, mist-ridden place. I know just how cold because in the winter of 1948 I worked there for the Crown. I worked in the company of Old Man Gibbs and Tommy Cinderby. Old Man Gibbs was Ernie Gibbs, a highly respected local resident and local preacher, father to Tom Gibbs the one-time headmaster of Steam Mills School. I don't know if Old Man Gibbs was really old - ie. older than I am now! - but he seemed it to me in my relative youth. During the war and just after, labour was so short that fit, elderly people carried on working. Ernie Gibbs was certainly as fit and able to do a steady day's hard work as the next man. He sustained the rigours of a day in the open, walking to and from his residence just above the Point Inn, without blinking an eyelid!

We were maintaining the newly-planted conifers that had recently replaced the mature trees of the Meend.

Tommy Cinderby was from Cinderford. His journey was further than that of Mr Gibbs being from Valley Road but I fancy he came part of the way by bus, a service which, in those days, by its frequency, presumed to benefit the community and not merely its shareholders ! Tom was not fit. He had a badly disabled arm from an old injury and it dragged him down. Poor old Tom battled on and took a draught of cider occasionally to keep his pecker up.

But Tom's value was in his fire-lighting skill. He could start a fire on the wettest, coldest, blowingest morning with - wait for it! - a Rizla cigarette paper and one match! This ability was of great pride to him. After all, wouldn't it have been easier to use half-a-box of matches and a piece of old fish and chip paper? No, Tom rationed himself to these two meagre aids and I see him now, kneeling low like a man in deep worship, weathered, green trilby pushed back off his forehead, tatty old mac wrapped around his thin body, blowing into life the tiny conflagration he had started. Before long we'd have a roaring, cheering fire by which to eat our bread and cheese and drink from bottles (no Thermoses then) still-warm, sweet tea - the bottles, corks loosened, simmering by the blaze.

Yes, in my mind's eye, I am taken back to 1948, crunching over rimed brushwood into an empty world of desolation and mist.

But the world is not empty. There, materialising like a tableau from a Victorian melodrama, two figures. They sit unmoving, one on an upturned log, the other on the stool of a felled chestnut. Ernie has his short-stemmed pipe clenched hard between his teeth in a sort of defiant resilience. From his lips come short, sharp violent snorts of smoke, bluer than the mist, which drift away in miniature clouds over the frosted undergrowth. Tom is hunched forward, drooping, his mac pulled about him, the pockets sagging with his tea bottle and his bread. He smokes one of his especially thin Ringers roll- ups made, in all likelyhood

...like a man in deep worship...

Like a tableau from a Victorian melodrama, two figures. They sit unmoving, one on an upturned log, the other on the stool of a felled chestnut.

from the stripped-out stubs of previous roll-ups. The only sound is the insistent hack of Tom's cough and an occasional bubble from Ernie's pipe.

This scene is etched on my consciousness, more an emotion than a happening. We would see no-one all day except perhaps a glimpse of Kenny Durham coming down the ride from Pit House with his whippet running ahead to start out the rabbits.

That winter got into my bones somehow - no, into my very soul. Perhaps it was the mystical quality of the Meend that did it. Here was a place with a thousand ghosts.

At the top end was a knoll with a clump of pine trees. Pingary's Tump is an enigma because it was Eli Hatton, not Pingary, who was hanged and gibbeted there in 1723 for murdering Thomas Twiberville of Mitcheldean. Who was Pingary? No authority seems to venture the answer. Was he the local hangman perhaps?

The trouble was, as Eli's corpse rotted on its rope, the myriads of flies it generated in the hot and humid summer of 1723 migrated to Mitcheldean and on market day, smothered the produce with their festering presence. These were the days of lurid superstition and it may have been the town folks thought it some form of retribution for being too hasty in turning off old Eli.

Whatever the truth, Eli Hatton perished there. Pingary, on the other hand, was the man who lent his name to this spot of morbid recollection. A small track wound from Wigpool past the gloomy pines of Pingary's Tump. *'Eli's Post',* the stump of the gallows was known and recognised even in Nicholls's time; it was a place to be avoided!

When courting his bride to be my son had to cycle after every visit, past the haunted spot on his way home. So anxious did he become each time he encountered the place that eventually, trying to whizz by in double-quick time, he dropped the slender wheel of his sports bike into a pot-hole and crashed. The bike was unrideable. He picked it up and ran down the road to the top of the Stenders Hill and afterwards had to face the long trek through Abenhall, through a darkening night, through Guns Mills and Flaxley to Elton. But Pingary didn't put him off and he married the maid!

The Tump has, in the between-years, become the site of a water-pumping station, built during the 1960s. It is, or used to be, enclosed and lit by dozens of mercury vapour lamps. I often wonder if the night-watchman, in the dead of his shift, doesn't sometimes hear the creaking of the gallows rope and, when reaching round for his sandwiches, finds them crawling with spectral flies!

Pingary and Eli had their brief day of fame - or infamy to be correct. More than three hundred years were to pass, the slow changing woodland at times as silent as the grave, at times disturbed by the trams rattling along the line from Wigpool Iron Mine to Fairplay and finally down to Broadmoor.

Then came the Yanks! Here they made their base the subject of which I have dealt with in a previous chapter.

Of recent years I have collected Penny Buns from the places where once the Yanks had their billets and cookhouses. Every time I leave the wood I pass the depression where an open-ended Nissen hut provided shelter on a wet day for my workmates and I. And sometimes I fancied I saw old Ernie Gibbs appearing through the mists of the past, sitting on a tree stump, chewing his pipe-stem in that particularly ferocious way.

No, Meend is for mystery, not for wasteland.

BOGUE

The period of World War II marked the drastic and sudden felling of the Georgian oakwoods. The Forest environment changed within a very short space of time. The skies were opened, where once had stood an unbroken canopy of oak. Where there had been leaves was open, rolling upland. You could once, for instance, have entered the green, dappled world of the pre-war Forest at Dunk's and walked without stepping out of the shade continuously until you emerged at Popes Hill. Going westward you could have done the same until you came out at Five Acres. After the war - no longer!

The timber was necessary for the War Effort and since it was pretty well mature, down it came before the axes and heavy equipment of the lumberjacks. I name the period the Great Felling for nothing before like it had ever occurred in the Dean. It was sudden and complete. True the carpetbagging of Sir John Winter had denuded the natural forest until, in the 16th and 17th centuries the area had become a *"howling wilderness"* as one surveyor put it. But this had been a slow, corrosive process extending over a longish period.

After the original ravishing of the natural forest, the effort to replant had been erratic and did not really get under way until the beginning of the 19th century. In any case, many of the trees planted were slow-growing, broad-leaved varieties. There was then a period of quiescence in the woods while the trees grew. By the war they were up to sixty feet high and ripe for the axe.

In the comparitively tranquil lands of the Crown therefore, there happened in 1939 or soon after, an upheaval of immense proportion.

Since most of the strong young males were drafted into the Forces, the labour force to deal with the demand in the woods was a rag-tag bunch recruited from all sorts of sources. There were old land workers, some of them brought out of retirement, there were young Land Army girls, conscientious objectors, unfit young men and above all, from my point of view, schoolboys brought in for the duration of their school holidays. This scene was of course a million miles from the appalling unemployment of the years immediately before. The national call went far beyond the current issues and rules of good economics. Not that these would prevail for long. We were to learn that the old-fashioned idea of thrift should be tempered. Payment of fair wages to the working man, elevating his credit-worthiness and encouraging him to spend would start and sustain the revolving of that huge wheel of economic growth we all now depend upon!

Gone were those agonising waits for the pit hooter to see if there was to be a shift, the pitiful wages, the industrial injury, the stagnation. Men were now to be drafted into the pits!

But I digress. In the woods on the west of the Dean the tatty labour-force I have described, was presided over by George Lees the Crown's Forester who lived in the holding at Edgehills Lodge high on the crest of the hill overlooking Abenhall and the Flaxley valley.

George Lees was one of those men whom, if you are lucky enough to encounter during your life, will have an infinite and profound influence upon your well-being and your life-pattern. He lives in my memory now, as large as life as he was in stature, striding the rides of his forest beat. He was a preacher of some ferocity and thumped the Bible at the tin chapel at Collafield. He was a good, gruff man of enormous strength and of huge humanity.

George Lees was no desk man. The pen-scratching he left to others, much to the chagrin of his Crown employers amongst whom he was renowned for his disinclination to the filling in of documents. But he was as big and long lasting as an oak and no-one challenged his integrity, least of all the autocratic Deputy Surveyor replete in plus-fours and tweeds and with a retinue of acolytes. They were formidable but not as formidable as George Lees himself. He, in his fine khaki uniform with big, stand-off pockets, flat cap, breeches and calf-leggings, green flashes on his cuffs and lapels, was a figure seemingly rooted in the forest around him; a green giant with a heart of gold.

Time-keeping among the Crown workers presented a problem scattered as they were through the length and breadth of some fifty square miles of forest. You were to be on the job at seven wherever the site might be. Since there was no public transport through the rides of the forest, this might involve a heathy trudge at an hour when most were only stirring. Distances could extend into several miles from home. It is said that during one period, the Jones brothers, renowned tree-fellers of Pope's Hill, walked daily, seven miles as the crow flies to, and seven miles from Ross Chase to do a day's felling. I calculate they were walking about four hours a day starting at 5 am and arriving home at 5 pm. It was indirectly, this factor that stimulated a direct confrontation between the axe men and George Lees - the only one I witnessed that ever got anywhere near being bad-tempered.

George Lees arrived at one site just before 3 pm. The fellers had, as usual, packed their tools away, slung their tommy bags over their shoulders and

The Alpha Man

were enjoying a last pipe of tobacco before starting the homeward trek. They made no move as the figure of the forester appeared over the horizon. He approached diffidently as always and when within speaking distance, loudly and gruffly intoned, *"An' what's all this then?"*

Not a word in reply came from the fellers. They remained fixed in their positions, eyes focused on the horizon, the only sound the occasional sucking on an old pipe and the only movement the manifestation of a puff of blue tobacco smoke drifting into the wind.

George Lees adopted his 'A' position. In this posture he presented a fairly terrifying picture; his boots planted firmly among the wood chippings, hands on hips, legs akimbo; his leather leggings glistened dully. Still no words were exchanged. But the challenge was not to be avoided. He represented a modern icon, A-alpha, the boss. We lesser mortals who had no pretentions to axe work, being there merely to collect up and burn the brushwood, scuffed our toes in the litter.

At long last, after what seemed an eternity, one of the older fellers took his pipe out of his mouth, spoke the raw, unbellished words, *"On th'axe you do finish at three o'clock,"* and put his pipe back in his mouth.

"Oh ho! I an't 'eard o' thick rule afore, mind," came the reply.

Another long pause. *"'as bin as long as I can remember,"* said the spokesman. Eyes never met.

The Forester circled slowly about the group somewhat like an enraged rhinoceros weighing up a knot of scared but recalcitrant tourists. There were long moments of pregnant silence.

Then, as if at an unheard signal, pipes were knocked out, roll-ups stubs thrown in the ash of the fire. The four swung their bags over their shoulders and were off across the cut without another word.

George Lees watched their disappearing figures, the wood, or what was left of it, swallowing them up in a kind of defiant silence. The Forester swung round on the rest of us.

"Well mind! You lot'd better get on wi' it an' stop a-gawpin'" he roared. We partook ourselves violently to our jobs.

So far as I know nothing more came of this incident. The axe men continued to leave at three and George Lees acknowledged their plea as by the logic rather than the rule. He kept his distance at the critical time. To me, as a young man, it was an illustration of the triumph of compromise without discussion!

George Lees lost no respect. After all, it represented his own avowed creed of the value of skill over bureaucracy; the cutters had had a distinct and unique advantage. How much good oak timber could be lost in the use of unskilled tree-fellers? To fell an oak using an axe and crosscut saw was a graceful art - destroyed nowadays by the demonic power saw.

The axe strokes fell, chipping out great and succulent wedges, each often too big to carry. They tipped out of the trunk as if they had been ordained to do so. When this represented a goodly bite, the great saw was placed against the bole. A man knelt down on each side and, slowly at first, gathering speed, the full length of the blade swung backwards and forwards until it created a huge, full-throated song of its own. The chippings sprayed in a shower at each stroke. The blade sank through the wood like a cheese-wire through best Cheddar. The men bent their backs to the swing until the first cracks were heard in the trunk. They eased their stroke, taking the saw gently through the last stages. The great tree creaked, the sound like agonising cries echoing through the wood. Then, ever so slowly, it began to topple, at first as in a dream then gathering momentum, culminating in a momentous crashing plunge.

The saw was retrieved neatly and without rancour as the tree toppled forward and the cut gaped at the rear. The cutters scrambled to their feet and stood back regarding the final fall with great respect as if the enactment of their work was of immense and sacred importance. Fred Jones would frequently I remember, push his cap back off his brow and clench his pipe,

A man knelt down on each side and, slowly at first, gathering speed, the full length of the blade swung backwards and forwards until it created a huge, full-throated song of its own.

which he had retained between his teeth during the whole operation, in some private act of homage.

There is no doubt that the felling of a great oak was an emotional moment and the fellers, as hard-boiled as they seemed, were duly affected. If there was any sort of apprehension in their faces however, it was because the trunk had fallen two inches out of the path designated for it; perhaps the breeze had twisted it ever so slightly as it fell. You couldn't fell a tree in a heavy breeze for instance.

The Jones's, it is said, could press a forked stake into the ground and fell a fully grown tree into the fork driving the stake into the ground. Anything short of this degree of success was considered a failure!

To all this skill, George Lees paid homage. And it is true, the men deserved their right. They would fell no more, no less trees in a working day sticking to a bureaucrat's idea of a working day. Today we have forgotten this principle. We are struggling to effect impossible targets in order to sustain economic growth. People are suffering great stress as a result. Mechanisation has disturbed the balance and destroyed the joy. The world's great natural timber resources are dwindling at an alarming rate. The fellers' power saws rant from dawn to dusk!

I could go on for ever with stories of George Lees, of his magnanamity, of his huge presence and his colossal patience. The men and boys working under him I am sure were never the same again.

Perhaps we were privileged people who were perverse to the traditional employment of the region working to shift times in the claustrophobia of the mines. We often saw no-one for day after day, the subtle, silent cracking of the summer vegetation and the hum of insects your only accompanying sound. In winter the rain, the wind and the ice were the boss. It gave me a lifelong addiction to cold, sweet tea, for cheese roasted in the flames of an open wood fire, for the burning feeling of heat from a roaring fire on a frosty day, for the unique taste of a fag smoked amongst woodsmoke, for the melancholy of rain beating upon fallen leaves, the satisfaction of utter exhaustion upon coming home at the end of a winter day, the smell of old woodsmoke on clothes, of cheese by the lump. It all got into my soul somewhere along the line.

George Lees too is in my soul. I hear his great bellow now, coming from the crest of Chestnuts Hill a full mile away as we played cricket on the grassy summer ride of The Jump when we should have been at work.

In his latter days, George Lees was a lollipop-man shuttling the schoolchildren across Belle Vue Road near the Wesley Chapel. No better lollipop-person could there have been, his sheer bulk and stolid shape a deterrent to any recklessly hasty motorist. I am told he would gaze fondly down on one or other of the bobbing heads or at the trusting eyes turned up towards him and would murmur, *"'ast 'ad thee egg this marnin'."*

Not any old egg - *"thee egg,"* your egg, that egg - the key to a simple, good, healthy life. Some writer with Saatchi and Saatchi might have made George a fortune!

My sincere thanks to Betty East neé Lees for permission to publish this tribute to her father.

THE PIPE THAT WOULDN'T GET LOST

The Forestry Commission, or the Crown as it was universally known by local people, employed a rich mixture of people during and just after the war. There were the very old on the one hand and the very young on the other. It was an interesting mixture.

Because of the manpower shortage, many fit men were in the Forces. The local Forester was able to recruit temporary labour in the form of holidaying schoolboys This was taken up with the utmost enthusiasm as a source of pocket-money.

The jobs we as youngsters were set, were in the main unskilled menial operations, though the planting of young trees required a modicum of skill and a certain amount of grit to stand up to the weather; planting was carried out during the winter.

One of the most congenial jobs was burning brushwood after the felling. We used to call it broush-burning. This needed patience, if not a certain degree of skill, in order to get a brushwood fire blazing on a cold, wet morning and to keep it going through thick and thin.

The trick lay in collecting the right quality of incendiary material - the right size and the right degree of dryness. Too damp, too large and too quick and you'd never get started.

Once you had your brush-fire started there was no problem. The following morning a stir-up of the ash would provide a glowing start for a handful of dry brushwood which would firstly begin to smoke in a most satisfying fashion, then burst into flame with almost an explosion of enthusiasm. A good bottom is essential in both fires and women was a quirky witticism I heard from one old Crown worker!

The broush fire had one particular problem. Since felling in the war was more or less continuous, much of the brushwood was green and sometimes bore green leaves. A very hot core was required to consume these and if you weren't careful even then, the leaves would burn off leaving a filigree of branches too open to support the flame. A great tower of hot, blackened branches would have to be dismantled and chopped up.

In frosty weather broush-burning was very pleasurable. The fires were enormous and so hot they roasted one's facing side till the buttons on your coat fairly burned your skin. Your face was constantly scorched and when you got home at night your eyes felt like dried-up marbles in sandy sockets. A minute or two in the armchair and you were asleep.

Broush burning invariably meant working alongside the axe-men. They had a placid, phlegmatic approach to life. One of them became a good friend. He was an inveterate pipe-smoker and indeed, to see his face less the pipe was like seeing a man ill-dressed. His briar was gripped between his teeth during all modes except eating. He could talk reasonably articulately with his pipe in his mouth. He worked on the crosscut with his pipe continuously in position though the contents were not always afire. On the axe however, the briar was tucked into his waistcoat pocket.

Fred's briar had a life of its own. A stubby, charred, stem-stained object it fitted in between his gripped teeth about two thirds along his mouth. It jutted a mere two and a half inches beyond his lips and was not unlike the pipe of Popeye.

Fred's was of a good knot of briar and, as I have said, the rim burnt to an uneven cornice of charcoal. In its blackened bowl he burned some pungent mixture of Ringer's Black Shag and Lord Knows What!

The most disconcerting thing was that it made him dribble. The act of bending down to the saw caused a plume of spittle to flow down the stem and, lifting according to the strength of the wind to stream off the bottom of the bowl in long, snake-like plumes. It did not pay to be on the leaward side of Fred in a stiff wind!

One day I ventured a complimentary comment about *"Fred's old pipe"*. He was noticeably flattered and pulled the object out of his mouth to regard it lovingly.

"Good old pipe, Fred," I ventured.

"Well oy." he replied reflectively. *"'Im's one o' two I bought at the' old shop at the bottom of the' 'ill. 'Er,* (the lady shopkeeper) *'ad several 'er got in some time afore the war - oh a dozen or more years agoo. The one split a'ter I'd 'ad 'n a few months. This un though,"* he turned the disreputable object affectionately several times in his fingers, *"this un - 'im a-lasted an' lasted."*

"You've done well to kip 'n," I suggested sharing his pride.

"Oy," said Fred, *"'Im's like a ship dog. 'Im do come back to tha when thee's want un - if thee bist lucky! Point is, everyone do know this 'ere pipe 'an if I do drop 'n or leave 'n lyin' about, thay as do find 'n do say, 'Surrey, there's old Fred's pipe', an'*

do bring 'n back. I daresay 'im 's come an' gone a dozen or more times like that." Fred replaced the pipe in his mouth a half smile of satisfaction on his weatherbeaten face.

Some time after in later life, I myself took to the pipe. I spent quite a lot of money on a series of fancy briars - long-stemmed, short-stemmed, curved-stemmed, pipes with built-in filters, pipes with stainless steel bases and unscrewable bowls, pipes with bulls' heads carved into the bowls. None lasted long and none seemed to get to that degenerate old age that Fred managed to achieve with his.

But it is a matter of perception. I had a friend once, a man of some temperamental leaning. He was an inveterate pipe smoker. I was with him in his car one day, driving along. The car was one of those old models with an open shelf under the dashboard. He reached down and scraped out his pipe from the awful debris and burnt tobacco, half-used tobacco packets and all sorts of other rubbish there. He deftly filled the pipe on the steering wheel, still driving. Fishing out a match he lit the filling puffing furiously until the visibility in the car was practically nil. I was used to this and it must be remembered that traffic on the roads was quite sparse in those days. We were on a quiet Welsh byroad.

All of a sudden he let out a great snort of rage, wound the window down and hurled the pipe with all his might into the passing countryside.

"What the blazes did you do that for?!" I asked with some alarm.

"It's gone," he rasped.

"I know it's gone," I replied. *"Out there somewhere and likely to start a fire."*

"No it's gone - like they all do eventually. They become clogged with all the charcoal and spit. There's nothing you can do about it. I've tried boiling them in caustic soda, reaming them out with hedgehogs, soaking them in rum. Nothing works. You might as well throw them away when they reach that stage. I do now."

His pipes were always the best quality expensive English briars. Fred would have considered the point of their discarding a mere beginning!

COOL WATERS

To work for the Crown was like no other form of employment that I can think of. It could be hard and monotonous but the benefits lay in the mode of the workplace itself - unlimited expanses of open air and greenery. Often one became totally swallowed up in it. In summer the silence seemed to be accentuated by the hum of insects. In winter it was the crackling of frost or the squelch of dead leaves beneath your boots you noticed. You yourself became a part of this amalgam of nature. There were few larger sounds to break the silence so it was the small ones to which you became attuned; the cracking of dry vegetation, the sighing of the wind in the boughs, the rattle of rain on leaves, the babbling of a woodland stream.

In the factories the noise boom had started and workers demanded constant *musac* to stimulate their effort. Music While You Work was the order of the day and this was the precursor (and what a curse?!) of the dreaded rock-playing transistor.

The variance between the factory floor and the woods was profound.

At *bread times* in the woods you threw yourself down amongst fragrant vegetation or you sat atop a log before a roaring fire. Sometimes you were in a magical place - some nook or dingle beyond the beyond, out of mind, out of sight, your presence virtually unrecorded.

Once I worked with a gang of other youngsters on a very steep woodland bank we aptly called *"The Jump"* near to St Anthony's Well. Now St Anthony's Well is a magical and mysterious place where a constant gush of ice-cold, crystal-clear water emerges from the hillside plunging into a pre-medieval, masonry-lined trough of quite large dimension. It was high summer and the task on hand was the cutting of bracken from around the young trees on the adjacent hillside. By lunchtime we were hot and dusty and our water bottles dry. It was the time to walk to the well to replenish them with this bitingly intense spring water. At the same time we lingered to eat our bread gulping huge mouthfuls of the stimulating water. Coming straight out of the Devonian roots of the Dean this water was cold enough to make your head sing. It flowed from a liverwort-encrusted grotto in the

As the seconds ticked by the icy cold penetrated the skins, reaching sinnew and bone. Sinnews began to quiver and go into cramps; bone began to ache.

bank, swirling and eddying troops of dead leaves towards the larger trough of anciently hewn rocks. The whole edifice nestled in a steep, cool bank beneath ancient beech trees.

Though we never immersed ourselves completely in the trough - the shock of the water would have doused our work incentive for the rest of the day! - we often sat around the stone parapet our hot feet dangling in the water. It had soon become clear that this was not a practice which could be indulged in at will. At first, the water was most pleasant. As the seconds ticked by the icy cold penetrated the skin, reaching sinnew and bone. Sinnews began to quiver and go into cramps; bone began to ache.

A competition started as to who could let their feet stay in the longest.

The ache escalated, the cramps increased their severity, the pain became rampant! Faces grimaced, bodies squirmed; hands grasped at knees, torsos rolled from side to side, teeth gnashed. Finally, with a swoosh the beaten tore their feet from the water and lay in agony gasping and groaning while the pain subsided to a thankful bearable level. The winner was of course the one who was the last out!

It took time for the feet to return to normal but when that point was reached they felt marvellous. Bearing mind the alleged curative properties of the Well, the members of that gang of workers have, to this day I imagine, the best feet in the County.

Watering places in and around the Dean were well patronised in the 1920s and 30s when seasides were too far distant to visit without great planning and the leisure time to do so. St Anthony's Well was one favourite place out of several and on a fine Sunday the spot would be surrounded by picnic parties.

St Anthony was a Fransiscan friar renowned as a finder of lost things. He was such a potent preacher that Sister Celestine of St Anthony's School tells me the fish came out of the water to hear him! His influence in the Forest is obscure; little has been written of him. But he has the Well and a local school dedicated to his memory. The Well, I have heard it said, is one of the best-kept secrets of the Forest. Today it is rarely visited. Still a place of great beauty and contemplative solitude it lies tucked away below the eastern bastion of the Dean under a grove of immense and ancient beeches.

Other renowned watering places in the Forest included the town of Newnham alongside the western bank of the Severn. Trippers were brought here by pony and trap or later on by motor coach and bathed in the treacherous waters of the river which toiled sinuously between shifting banks of sand.

The Biblins, a beautiful spot in the Wye gorge below Symond's Yat where a strip of grassy pastures line the base of the steep valley was another though less accessible spot for bathing. A number of other places along the Wye were also frequented - Bishopswood, Huntsham Bridge and Ross-on-Wye itself. All offered relatively safe bathing stretches though having said so, drownings were regular occurrences.

More offbeat places in local brooks were found by the children. A partricularly well-visited place was the so-called Cannop Lido. This was actually the concrete lined cooling pond to Cannop Colliery. It received the pumped-out colliery water before this entered the Cannop Brook. The water was pleasantly luke-warm for reasons which I have never been able to ascertain. It was directed into the "Lido" via a long concrete sluice delivering a constant cataract to the upper end of the tank. The brook too entered the top end of the tank which was about three feet deep. A sliding sluice gate at the lower end of the tank retained the level.

"The Lido" is still there opposite the old colliery entrance. It is now almost completely full of silt brought down by the brook. Its days as a swimming pond were terminated when typhoid spores were identified in its waters. It is true to say that we all bathed in this water blithely unaware of the danger. Furthermore, the water contained a high degree of the finest, black silt. In the course of swimming this attached itself to the pre-adolescent hairs around the chin and one emerged with a sooty beard, an effect much sought after by the youths of the day!

Today the Lido is a neglected eyesore, neither ancient nor modern and without its adjacent mine buildings to give it authenticity. It is not economically welcome yet no one seems to have the nerve to dispense with it. It remains therefore, caught in limbo yet ostracised except by the occasional kingfisher which flashes above its sombre blackness, the grey wagtails which bob along its concrete parapet or the pied flycatchers which chime from the oaks overhead.

In a way the Lido symbolizes the current state of the Dean, a compromise between the old, fading industrial landscape and the new, managed woods. Strangely, neither are fulfilled. The industrial heritage - the decaying buildings, the slag heaps, the broken-down masonry, the discarded corrugated iron, the poverty-ridden homes, the railways - have been ruthlessly removed, at least where they impinged conspicuously upon the public eye. Deeper into the roadless tracks some remain. In the grown oaks along Cannop Bottom where pits crowded from Brierley to Parkend, one can occasionally find a surprising memorial of the activities here where a steel cable snakes up amongst the branches of grown trees, carried there by sheer casual passage of time. Strange pot-holes and mounds are scattered through remote woods where drifts and shafts once existed. But you would have to get off the beaten track to find them now.

In the 1940s this environment was predominantly industrial but the woods were softening it all. Woodland paths winding for miles between trees used to be marked with white patches of spent carbide where the homing miners knocked out their acetylene-driven lamps, always in the same place each day. Some future archaeologist will unearth these little white mounds and wonder why they are here!

We the Crown workers could sit and eat our bread in the clear air and listen to the distant clang of the bond at the few remaining collieries.

WARTS AND ALL

The old Forest was self-sufficient. Within its boundaries used to be the total requisites to sustain a simple life, not to the point of opulence but to the point of sufficiency.

Amongst the essential provisions and in the absence of an effective medical service, the inhabitants had their own traditional medical dispensation conducted by recognised appointees of the art of easement and cure. Such characters handed down their skills from generation to generation. They were mostly woman and their status in the community was generally prefixed with the title 'Mother'. Everything from unwanted pregnancy to boils or the flux might come under the scope of the local Mother.

The emergence of state financed medicine for all gradually did away with the community practitioners but the more long-lived of them persisted in a modest way until well after the war.

Within the repertoire of these old-time homeopaths were practices which frankly bore the mystical nature of faith healing. Now I am a sceptic - the natural outcome of an education directed towards science and a suspicion, if not a rejection of the paranormal.

In my teens and through into my twenties, my fingers, in particular those of my right hand, became contaminated with warts. I use the term contaminate advisedly for there is no evidence that warts are acquired from any external influence, germ, virus or parasite. They arise from some internal waywardness of the cells causing them to go off on independent sprees of their own. My warts appeared firstly in the form of an odd but isolated individual. This one acquired a colleague and gradually they proliferated, often merging in groups, until the skin of my hand and in particular my index finger, was obscured. They were of the coarse type which somewhat resemble barnacles having round open tops filled with small grey, tightly-packed protruberences. If they split, they could be very painful.

The matter was becoming inconvenient. Dr Sumption was still in practice but recalling the unfortunate encounter from my days of acne, I sought the advice instead, of a doctor in the distant town where I attended college.

He was a jolly man, a sympathetic man, displaying a bedside manner far from the severe, indifference of old Sumption. He looked at my hands and sucked his lip.
"Bad, Mr Christian. So many of them. I can refer you to a surgeon, or I can prescribe a caustic agent you paint on day and night and if you are persistent, will eventually, literally, burn them off. There again ... with so many ...", he turned my hands over and regarded them with a look of restrained agony on his features, *"... it will be painful!"*

There was a pause. He frowned. *"Then again ... You'll be going home for the long vacation next week. You live in the country don't you? Do you know any wart charmers?"*

I could hardly believe my ears. I'd heard of mysterious practices like rubbing warts with bacon and burying the bacon immediately. When it rotted, the warts, it was said, *"dropped off"*. I could not conceive, and was vastly interested to witness my many warts *"dropping off"* - raining down upon the ground like redundant ticks! It was a nice idea but I'd never tried it. Yet here was a medical man, a man of strictly secular training, apparently about to recommend some such unscientific voodoo!

"Wart charmers ...But ..."

The doctor looked amused. *"You're sceptical,"* he said. *"But believe me, I've a number of patients on my books who have responded to a charmer. Give you the name of a local one if you like but best you find your own at home. It's a case of local faith and sympathy I believe."*

I thanked him and promised to try though I must say I had little faith that he was doing other than avoiding the responsibility of a difficult treatment.

"Wouldn't be surprised to see you here next term sans warts," he exclaimed cheerfully. He jumped to his feet and saw me out.

I came home to the Dean and took vacational job with the Crown.

"Thee's wanna goo an' see ol' Dick," suggested a workmate. *"'Im a' charmed dozens as I do know of."*

Dick lived on Popes Hill. A retired tree-feller he was one of four local brothers all famed for their home-produced cider. He lived with his wife in a

small-holding right at the end of the track over the hill. His old-fashioned cottage was surrounded by orcharding and as pretty an idyll as you might find the length and breadth of the land.

Dick's cider (dare I say it even now!) was the most renowned of the four brothers. When it comes to cider-making, the competition puts chrysanthemum or marrow growing in the shade! Cider-making was not just a country activity, it was a religion. Drinking it was as robust an activity as making it and there was deep ritual involved.

Dick was renowned as a wart charmer as well as being a dispenser of straight speaking and even straighter country home truths. I approached his cottage with some trepidation.

As I drew near I could see he had apparently anticipated my arrival and was leaning over the gate his shirt sleeves rolled up to the elbows. His moleskin breeches were held up taught with stout leather braces. His long, weather-beaten face and whispy white hair was exactly as you would anticipate. His elbows were lodged between the pales of the gate and his hands clasped in front.

"'Ow be you?" he said.

"I 'm fine - apart from these warts," I said, deciding that a direct, no-nonsense approach was the right one.
Dick did not acknowledge the warts or their presence in the state of things.

"Come along in," he said. *"We'd better go into the surgery."*

The surgery?! What was I hearing?!

He swung the gate open and stood aside for me to enter. We walked around the cottage on a worn flagstone path and into a spacious back kitchen which formed a lean-to to the house. The massive rubble stone walls were coated with years of limewhite, the roof supported on beetle-riddled beams, of fine old clay pantiles. The flagstone path continued inside to form the floor, a venerable and rickety door of wide aperture scraped closed in a bleached frame. A tiny cobweb-filled window punctured the thick wall at the far end; shaded by external shrubbery, it imparted no significant light to the interior. It was cool in here - as cool as a summer morning.

Still no mention of warts.

"Do y' like a drop a' cider?" he asked.

"Why yes," I said hesitantly.

Dick reached into some dark, dust-ridden recess in the wall and drew out what appeared to be a small beaker of opaque, grey material. From this, with a sharp puff, he blew the accumulation of chaff, spiders and their derivatives. He handed me the vessel. I saw it was not very large, holding perhaps ten ounces, and of a curious mottled appearance. It was indeed the ritual horn cup from which all home-brewed cider must be partaken.

I went over to the barrel and knelt before it as if praying for its goodness.

In the shadows of the shed, mysterious and huge like a row of carved Egyptian kings I saw there were five immense barrels. They stood on their ends upon a stone plinth and were tapped near the bottom rim each with a wooden tap.

Dick indicated the row of barrels.

"Now you a' gotta choose thee own. Thay be all different years ar blends. One's a good 'un, tothers be alright - but I shan't tell thee which is the good 'un." His face was deadpan. This was no matter for joking. I realized there would be no clues or help. I stood or fell by my choice. I knew instinctively that he would not tell me even, if I had chosen the good 'un.

"I'll .. er .. I'll have that 'un over there." I indicated the third barrel from the far end.

Dick gave not a flinch or murmur. His face remained completely impassive. He said, *"Well, goo an' 'old thee cup then."*

I went over to the barrel and knelt before it as if praying for its goodness. I held the cup below the straight peg of the tap and Dick came over and turned it gently.

Have you ever seen vintage cider deliver from a wooden tap? There is something indeed mysterious about it. As the handle turns there is a slight pause, then the liquid trickles in a thin, heavy line at first. The trickle increases in volume but not so much as to exceed a slow, bubble-free, unbroken surge. There is no hiss merely a strange rustling noise as the liquid strikes the horn cup.

The level of the liquid in the shadowy depths of the cup increased miraculously. The colour was the most fugitive pale green. It was as clear as spring water and completely flat.

Dick closed the tap when the liquid was near the rim. It was then his face took on a pleased expression. It was like an absolution; he was the priest and had delivered something akin to spiritual relief. I still had no idea whether I had the good or the not so good cider! But one thing was sure, the not so good was good enough! He took none himself.

I stood up feeling somewhat awkward in my solitariness. Dick watched me expectantly and obviously required me to drink. I drank.

Now I don't know just how to describe the sensation this simple act imparted. Looking back over the fifty-odd years that have now interceded I may have built up wrong or wishful impressions. But I reckon if I could put it adequately into words I would have made a fortune in advertising.

As the liquid hit the back of my throat there was a physical impact, a zing, an electric shock which started in my eardrums and whizzed around my semi-circular canals like particles in molecular fission. I had a sense of this utter and absolute spring-gin-mint-lemon-cold, thing. It left my Adam's apple bouncing on a sea of rip-roaring arctic waves.

The cup took only about three mouthfuls and was replenished from the same barrel of my original choice. No second chance!

The roaring of the arctic waves was now sinking to my legs, warming as it went.

"Come on in the parlour and meet the wife," said Dick as if knowing the feeling of leg fatigue cider imparts.

He replaced the horn cup without rinsing it. We walked to the house along the flagstone path.

His wife was a dignified Edwardian lady in a broad twill skirt seated by the black-leaded range which glowed in a way only those old-fashioned ranges could glow. She looked as if she had been sitting there waiting for me to come in. Her tiny hands were in her lap and her equally tiny feet in black, shiny shoes peeped out from beneath her skirts. Her back was dead straight and she sat in a formal upright posture. Her hair was snow white but the most striking thing about her face was her eyebrows which I recall, were bushy, but above all, black.

She nodded to my greeting and indicated for me to sit down in an old padded armchair opposite. Dick parked himself in a wheelback chair to the side of the door his elbows resting on his knees.

His wife enquired about my family, what part of the Forest they came from, how and why I came to be working for the Crown. To each answer she nodded politely adding no comment to prolong the subject. She said Dick had retired a few years ago but did not miss regular work since he had the holding and a few sheep.

"Ay - the Crown do miss I more 'n I do miss thay", he interjected with uncharacteristic humour.

No mention was made of warts. I began to realise it was part of the ritual.

Dick's wife eventually nodded more emphatically than before and I felt I had sort of been vetted. The contact was over. I rose and thanked the lady. She nodded and smiled and Dick got up and walked out ahead of me. We proceeded together to the gate which he unlatched and swung open allowing me to pass through while he leaned on the pales.

It was only then that he said, *"Let's 'ave a look at thay warts then."* The 'a' was short as in parts or tarts. I proferred my hands spreading the fingers. He took both by the wrists glancing almost casually then turning them, doing the same on the inside, for although the palms were clear, one or two of the unsightly growths were on the insides of the fingers.

"Thay'll goo," he said releasing my wrists. *"Thay'll goo - but thee's got to ferget about 'em. The longer thee's kip a-worryin' about 'em, thay'll stay. There was a mon who come to I some time back. 'Im 'ad one on the back on 'is neck - a big bugger! Six wiks later 'im come back an' said, 'This 'ere wart byunt gone.' Oy, I said, an' thee's know why? Thee's kip a-feelin round the back o' thee neck to see if 'im's still there. As long as thee's kip a-doin' that 'im'll oblige tha!"* Dick chuckled and sniffed wiping his forearm along his nose. *"I told 'n, thee's got to ferget about 'n an' when 'im caun't find thee fingers a-prying round there backuds and foruds, 'im'll goo. Not too long a'ter that I sid this 'ere mon. 'Im said to I, 'Thee wast right, 'im a gone. I put it out a' my mind, then one day the missus said, 'Thee warts gone!'"*

This was the longest speech Dick had made the whole time but the point was made.

"Someone told me you would have to count them," I said.

"No need. Thay'll goo," he repeated.

I thanked him, shook hands and asked, *"What do I owe you?"*

He shook his head fiercely with something akin to shock on his features. *"'Twunt work fer payment,"* he said.

I walked from the cottage in the afternoon sun and shrugged; so that was it! A non-event. Well, nothing lost.

I don't know what I expected. For a while I inspected my hands, feeling somewhat guilty that I was doing the very thing that was forbidden. Would the offending growths shrivel to a crisp then fall off in that time-honoured description? The warts persisted there, coarse and ugly.

Perhaps it was the prospect of returning to college which preoccupied me. Anyway, I had other things on my mind and the warts took second place. Three weeks, perhaps four, had passed. It was a few days before going back. It wasn't a member of the family who drew attention to the loss, it was merely myself. They were suddenly, completely, every man jack , not there! Whether they were there the night before, two days before, the hour before, I cannot say, because of course, they were out of my mind! The fact was, my fingers were pristine, the dozen or fifteen crater-like protruberences had been replaced by good, unmarred flesh! A miracle? An impossibility? You tell me!

A friend of mine who witnessed the warts in place and afterwards not in place, was astounded but tried to shrug it off.

"Must have been something in that cider," he said with the same sort of casual confidence that people put on when they haven't a clue. *Something in the cider?* - what on earth in the cider that could possibly be known to get rid of warts? True there was probably all sorts of unusual compounds in that very fine cider but none likely to have a purgative effect on warts.

No, the ritual of the cider was, I believe merely fulfilling the need to get acquainted, in the same way that my formal introduction to Dick's wife was a part of the process. It involved also, my tacit agreement to abide by the polite rituals, of partaking of the cider, of imparting my family history and I was aware of having been vetted for my integrity.

Be all that as it may, my feelings of elation were enormous. The warts had gone and indeed have never come back. I have acquired other warts - those brownish spots which come with age, those fleshy Devil's teats which respond to a tightly tied horsehair and other vague types of skin blemishes, but none of those dastardly craters.

I returned to college. The drama of the event I felt justified taking up a few minutes of the doctor's time, so I attended his evening surgery. Seated before him, I said nothing, just held out my hands.

"Marvellous," he said, *"but I won't say I told you so."*

"But doctor, how do you reconcile this with your professional practices?"
His smile broadened. *"Mr Christian, when my profession has the answer to everything, we shall have God upon His knees. I don't think it's likely to happen."*

I hope not!

BEES FOR THE ASKING

Working in the woods in summer you had to come to terms with the insects. The fairly innocuous wood flies pestered sweat-encrusted skin and a frond of bracken was useful as a fly whisk. More sinister flies in June and July were the blood-sucking horse-flies which came in several varieties the largest an inch long - as big as a hornet!

The horse-fly bite is administered through a short, blunt, horn-like probiscis. It makes a substantial puncture and at the same time injects infected saliva that causes the real damage. Like close relative the notorious Tsetse Fly of Africa it locates the host by its movement. Stand still and it may pass you by; working with your shirt off provides a tempting target!

Fortunately, Dean woods were relatively free of such insects unlike, for instance the peat moors of the North where I have been attacked by clouds of clegs - the smaller variety. Horse- flies attack when the sun is out. They mysteriously disappear if the sun goes behind a cloud.

At the top of the hate list for the Crown worker was however, wasps. The height of the wasp season is August and September which coincided with the weeding of the young plantations. Since many varieties of wasps make their nests in cavities in the ground it was inevitable at such time, that worker and wasp would come into confrontation. Such occasions were amusing to watch - less so for the participants!

The first indication that you had cut over a nest was probably the vague idea that the volume of flying insects about you had increased; there seemed to be a certain purposeful intensity in their movements. The next would be a burning stab on some exposed part of the body followed quickly by another and another. Examination at a glance of the trouser legs would show scores of doubled-up, yellowish shapes implanted in the material. It was no time to linger! Wasps are persistent; they like to see their tormentors well out of the vicinity. They follow and they attack even at tens of yards from their nest. Some crawl into the clothing and sting when they reach bare skin. The smoothness of their stings allow them to repeat the dose several times. Divestation of clothing is the only recourse. I have seen grown, tough men running for their lives throwing off garment by garment as they retreated until down to their underpants and then run farther! - and pause yet again to beat their flesh like monks in mortification!

"I'll climb the tree and thee 'old the box under the swarm

Wasps do not produce honey. Their survival through the winter is vested in the hibernating zeal of several giant queens who carry the many eggs of the new year's colonies in their bodies.

Bees on the other hand store the sugary product made from the nectar of flowers in order to feed their number over the winter. It is the honey that makes them commercially valuable. Bees swarm in the summer when a newly hatched queen decides to leave the hive taking a retinue with her. In its search for a new home the swarm moves from place to place, resting occasionally upon some common object which may happen to be convenient.

Stan was a big, enthusiastic forest worker with a constant smile and a stature to match his heart. He was working with Bert one summer near Greenbottom. Close by was the home of a smallholder whose plum orchard stretched up the bank towards the forest inclosure. It was a hot day. On calling at the smallholding for a replenishment of their drinking water, Stan and Bert noticed a swarm of bees had settled in a plum tree on the edge of the orchard. The bees were clustered in a great bunch which hung from the end of a small branch some eight feet up.

At the thought of five pounds for the swarm Stan begged a cardboard box from the smallholder.

"It be easy," he told Bert. *"All we 'ave to do is for I to climb the tree and thee 'old the box under the swarm. I'll cut the twig with my penknife an' they'll drop off into the box. Close the flaps an' we a-got 'em. We'll go 'alf an' 'alf."*

Bert had some trepidation but he obediently offered up the box as Stan climbed the tree.

"Bist ready?" shouted Stan.

"Oy," said Bert balancing the box on the palms of his upturned hands beneath the black, seething swarm.

A couple of bees dropped off and landed on Bert's shirt collar; another got tangled in his hair. It was too much! He dropped the box and beat his head. The bees took umbrage!

In the tree Stan was about to cut the twig. Too late, he realised that many of the bees were detaching themselves from the main mob and were searching for those who were tormenting them. Bert was already fleeing towards the sanctuary of the garden shed, a haze of bees in pursuit. Stan was not so lucky. He had to get down out of the tree. By the time he had done so and reached the garden shed he was well-and-truly plastered with angry bees.

Bees do not sting several times. Their stings are furnished with a barb which hooks into the flesh rendering the attacking bee doomed but in its death throes continuing to pump poison into the victim.

The many stings Stan received poisoned the whole of his system and he shortly broke out in a terrible affliction of sores. This however, did nothing to affect the sunshine of his character and he displayed the painful looking gatherings on his arms and legs with some pride as the battle wounds of the encounter. He recovered completely.

Bees are honourable warriors. On my mantlepiece is a china vase. It bears a shield surrounded by a wreath and scroll. The shield is emblazoned with three bees around a hive and the scroll bears the script *'Adversum mel'*. This is the crest of the town in Northern France where in 1915 during the Great War so many men of the Gloucestershire Regiment were lost in the Battle of Loos. The vessel was presented to me by the Town Mayor of Vermelles after the ceremonial replanting of the cherry tree at *Lone Tree* nearby, on the site of the old front line where the Gloucesters had fought.
The crest on the vessel depicts a victory over barbarian invaders when the townspeople, famous for their honey, set their enraged bees upon the attacking soldiers. Mel means honey. It was in this incident that the town acquired its name Vermelles whose literal meaning I do not have but I imagine means *true honey*.

Never underestimate bees!

Chapter 3

LEGENDS

TOM'S DOG

The following story is based on a true one. There are those living who will recognise it. I have altered the Christian names for reasons of deference. If I have provided some embellishment, it is with a sense of humility in demonstrating the fact that none of us are certain what this life is all about or what exists beyond the clouds.

The late afternoon drew to its close. The shrivelled light moved seamlessly from one shade of coppery grey to a more intense one of charcoal. The thaw, sustained by a slight rise in temperature at noon, ceased to drip from the trees and the thud of moist snow from the fir branches ceased altogether. The cold of approaching night gripped like a steel band crushing the landscape and all within it.

The old man came along the forest ride moving very slowly beneath the trees. His threadbare greatcoat was hunched high upon his shoulders, the collar turned up to the edge of his cap. He carried a small bundle in one hand, a hessian sack roughly rolled about some object. From this, dangling by a piece of coarse string, were a few sprays of holly. The old man's other hand gripped a longish thumbstick with which he steadied his stride. Both hands were gloveless but the fingers, short-nailed and scarred, protruded from the frayed edges of some woollen garment he wore beneath his coat. The pocket of his coat furthest away from the steady swing of his stick, was greatly expanded and from the open flap protruded the neck of a large, glass flagon sealed by a screw-in stopper.

Exactly a yard behind his heel followed a dog. It imitated the old man's posture exactly. Its head was drawn down into its neck-ruff, its gait slightly unsure but persistent.

Both imparted an image of great loneliness in the snow-ridden backdrop of this winter evening, the only living creatures within several miles. They made their way through the fading light towards some seemingly unlikely goal here in the wild wood.

The dog was a lurcher, or at least of that ilk. Its grizzled coat was thin and patchy and of that indeterminate natural tone known as agouti. Its longish, untidy tail was carried in a drooping loop almost brushing the snow.

The man stopped occasionally as if to gather his breath. When he did so the dog stopped too, remaining, head bowed, exactly a yard behind him. The old man would draw his sleeve across his nose using the arm which carried the stick which in turn, dangled like a pendulum, still clutched in the hand. The dog seemed to know the time this operation would take for at the end of seven or eight seconds it would raise its head perceptively and, although you could not see its eyes, you knew it was weighing up those tiny, almost imperceptible signals which would start them off again upon their hesitant journey.

Eventually, after what seemed a long time, when the cavities beneath the trees had become black, inscrutable voids and a distant owl began to hoot, the old man turned off the main ride along a tiny but well-worn path. It led to a glade among the trees.

Here, inconspicuous behind a tumble-down wall of mossy stones and amongst a gathering of lesser trees and bushes, loomed the barely discernible outlines of a cottage.

This was no man-dominated residence. It seemed indeed to be none other than a part of the woodland around it. What had been man-produced was tempered by the elements of nature.

The ancient lime-washed walls were grey with scale and in places green with algae. Here and there the crude stucco had cracked and fallen away revealing rough stonework unworthy of the name of masonry. The random stones were coarsely bonded with joints of crumbling mortar. The rusty guttering meant to carry rainwater clear of the walls, existed only where it had fallen away or hung down in untidy, pointless disorder. The slated roof was partly obscured by ivy and the foliage of crowding trees. The paintless windows were dim recesses in the outer structure, grey with grime and cobwebs, dejectedly covered with ragged lace curtains.

The house was not so much suffering from decay as being totally taken over by the natural elements surrounding it.

The broken gate, a mere token in the collapsing front wall, clung to its post by a single rusty hinge so that to open it the style had to be lifted and scaped over the tussocks of coarse grass and moss which threatened to engulf the path.

The man stopped before the gate and opened it having to lean his staff against the wall in order to get both hands free. His bundle he balanced on the top stone of the wall. The dog waited patiently at his heel. He entered and scraped the gate shut allowing the dog to enter and circle his legs. He bent unsurely and retrieved a large iron key from beneath a brick concealed in the weeds to the side of the front door. Eventually he succeeded in unlocking and pushing open the door. It was completely dark inside and there was a stale smell of dampness, old well-worn clothes and smoke.

The front door opened directly into a parlour from which a rickety staircase led off, bounded by a partition of brown matchboarding. The vague shapes of a bare, scrubbed table and a few other scraps of furniture were dimly visible. Leaning his stick against the door jamb, the old man stumbled over to the fireplace, placed his bunch of holly on the mantle shelf and groped for a box of matches he knew lay there. He bent and collected an armful of spruce brushwood from a heap which was piled in the shadows, kicked the cone of grey ash in the hearth to one side and threw the brushwood there. He struck a match and set it to the kindling. In a moment the flames sprang, crackling through the filigree of twigs, casting a dancing, flickering magic-lantern show, adding new dimensions to the objects in the room - an old dresser with some ruined china, a collapsing ladderback chair or two, an armchair seemingly covered with sacking; a brass oil-lamp on the table was a particular highlight.

The dog stood patiently soaking up the heat. Its eyes now glinted from beneath the brows of rough hair, reflecting the bursts of flame. The old man moved to the table and lit the battered oil-lamp. He turned up the wick which gave a more even light to the room and all within it. It was still devastatingly cold. He returned to the door, kicked it shut and shot the great iron bold into the jamb.

By the time he returned to the fireplace the kindling was well alight. He rummaged amongst the heaps of fuel which lay in the corner retrieving two great chips of oak. These he placed with care, one lodged against the other in a sort of tent, in the midst of the blazing spruce, scarcely bothering when the flames licked his hands.

He grunted with satisfaction and leaned, his body supported on his forearm along the mantlepiece his other hand held out in appreciation towards the chuckling, spluttering flames. The dog stood near, now steaming slightly; the smell of its damp coat pervaded the room. Both man and beast were caught there in an ancient tableau - a classic scene of survival; man and flame against a freezing wilderness.

As the flames grew the room assumed a sumptuousness it did not really possess.

The old man sank into the armchair exhausted. The dog stood quietly near. It too soaked in the welcoming blaze, feeling the heat penetrating between the dusty curls of its coat.

The wood crackled and spit and a glowing fragment was tossed in a flaming arc onto the dirty rag rug which covered the boards in front of the hearth. The dog stood back sharply but not in panic.

"There's my boy", growled the man. *"That'll warm thee cockles wun it?"* He sniffed again and wiped his nose clear. He stretched out his foot and stamped on the glowing ember, controlling the fire as mankind had learnt to do years past.

The scene was as familiar to Tom as it was welcome. Yet it was special this evening. It was Christmas Eve. He'd been out toiling in the forestry and though it was barely 4 o'clock in the afternoon he'd come through the fading light to the darkened and broken cottage beside the stone-walled paddock.

He'd called in at the public house on the edge of the town for his quart of cider and for a chicken left there by his friend for him to collect. The chicken was in the hessian sack. He remembered the holly and struggled to his feet picking up the little bundle of needle-sharp leaves and red berries, setting it somewhat precariously behind a small, framed picture.

The dog stood for a minute enjoying the fire then moved to its bed, an old jacket lying beside the hearth. It slumped down with a grunt and laid its muzzle on its paws.

* * * * * * * * * * * *

Tom suddenly felt overwhelmed with tiredness. He had come back to work in the forest because the Forestry people wanted his skill in the wartime. In truth his age was against it but the work gave purpose to his day.

Before he plucked and drew that chicken he'd have a minute or two. Without discarding his coat he lay back in the armchair. Wisps of steam began to rise from his boots and trouser legs. The heat seeped through his body and his eyes went out of focus so that he saw only the red and yellow dancing lights through the partly closed lids.

A woman in a print pinny, her hair tied up in a bun, smiled from the porch.

The world shrank, concentrated into this one warm, comfortable spot with his whole being in the centre of it. The blackness and the harshness outside was completely irrelevent. Here, he was home and dry for the umpteenth time - ready for anything else life had to offer. Tomorrow was Christmas Day. He'd cook his chicken and enjoy it with a glass of cider, split some logs maybe and collect some more brushwood. Later he'd walk to the pub to replenish his cider.

He felt drowsy. The room danced with homely reflections.

He must have dropped off. He had this irrepresible desire to open his eyes.

Alice stood there just to the side of the fireplace, smiling at him. She stretched out her hand. The dog got up and went to her wagging its tail, licking her hand with affection.

Tom exclaimed, *"Alice!,"* a note of pleased surprise in his voice. It was, after all, five years since he had seen her last. He had said goodbye to her upstairs in the bedroom which he had never entered since save to see her carried away.

"Tom," she said, *"it's time!"*

"Alice!" he repeated, *"I never thought....! But I've missed you."*

"I know," she said. She smiled again, the same warm smile he had known and carried in his heart.

Tom closed his eyes. There was a huge joy welling up in his throat. He'd been so lonely all these years.

* * * * * * * * * * * *

Frank said to his mate, *"I don't know where old Tom's got to. It's not as if 'im 'ad much to do other than to come back to work."*

It was Monday, the first after Christmas weekend. The foresters were back at work.

The following morning, Tuesday, there was still no Tom.

"Come on," said Frank, *"we'd better goo an' see what's 'appened to th' old bugger. 'Im might a' bin on the cider."*

They rode their bicycles through the freezing woods to the cottage and saw it to be cold and deserted.

Frank burst through the door, the bolt splintering out of the frame. Tom was in the armchair, slumped back, his eyes closed, a look of great peace on his face. His one arm hung down with the hand extended as if he had held it out before he died.

The dog got up off its sack and wagged its tail recognising Frank and his mate.

"Surrey! Wha's think!" exclaimed Frank. *"'Im a bin locked in 'ere for three days wi' old Tom - a-starvin'! - an' thick there chicken on the table. But 'im 'a'n't touched a scrap!*
"Come on o' boy. Thee's better come wi' I."

The dog walked to him and buried its head in his trouser leg.

Frank looked around the room. *"We'd best leave put for the coroner."*

They left solemnly. The dog fell in behind Frank. They walked their bicycles through the winter woods.

* * * * * * * * * * * *

When I met Frank at his work some time after, he was eating his bread. The lurcher was curled up silently on an ancient, tattered jacket. I made to approach but was greeted by a warning growl and a curl of the lip.
"Dosn't goo near 'n. 'Im'll 'ave tha! 'Im's guardin' Tom's jackut. But 'im's alright wi' I." Frank stretched out his hand and scratched the animal's ear.

"I reckon 'im's a-waitin'," Frank said after a pause.

Waitin' for Tom

"Waiting?" I asked.

"Oy, a-waitin' fer Tom. Till then 'im do put up wi' I!" Frank laughed with that rasping, bronchial laugh of his.

Tom's cottage no longer stands. It had been aforest lodge of the older vintage and had come to the end of its years. After Tom it was just allowed to decay until the roof went then the walls were pushed in and the combustible debris burnt.

I often go to where it stood. But there are bramble humps all over the garden and the little paddock is almost obscured with mole hills and nettles. The site is almost unrecognisable as having once been a house in which people lived their lives.

One day, a still, sunny afternoon, I was passing. I looked across the moss-grown stones. They, like the garden and paddock were overgrown with a riot of briars; but the ellemblough which grew by the privy persisted incongruously in the lea of the forest trees.

As I gazed, I saw the cottage recreated. But the walls were upright, the garden gate not falling off its hinges! The windows were painted and there were bright curtains in them. I fancied I saw Tom leaning on his spade in the neatly cultivated garden. A woman in a print pinny, her hair tied up in a bun, smiled from the porch. On the path frolicked a young and playful pup.

I blinked and it was gone!

All kinds of thoughts ran through my mind in explanation. Was this just a vision of wishful thinking? Or was it some demonstration of relativity? Perhaps, on that still, breathless day, when time seemed of no consequence, I had broken through the fragile screen which separates our lives from the past. After all, to someone looking in from twenty light-years away, they'd see the very scene I had described. It is only a man-made concept of time which separates past and present.

Perhaps reality is that it's all happening together, no time, just a blink in the eye of God.

THE HANGING TREE

The oak grew on the edge of the forest not far from the village of Drybrook. It stood just off the main road surrounded by trees of much lesser stature. A short track led to it, made in part by those who had ventured out of their way to admire its venerability. From this you will gather it was no ordinary tree.

A sapling when the first Elizabeth succeeded to the throne of England in 1558, it matured during her reign. It survived the great storm of February 1662. Its omnipresence upon the landscape had lasted for close on four hundred years. Even those lesser plants which surrounded it seemed to stand back in awe. No mere striplings themselves, they yet surrendered space and respect. Or was there something else? Did they not seem to lean back from it almost as if in horror!?

The tree's age was reflected in its form. It rose out of the ground extruding itself in a great surge towards the light. It resembled a vast cry, a cry of triumphant survival. Its trunk was sculpted in gnarled columns like ten trunks inseperably joined; upon its surface were scars and horn-cags and tumours and rents and pocks and lesions, a veritable panorama in which lived a multitude of creeping things. Its girth was near to fifteen feet.

This huge trunk was not a thing of symmetry. It did not match lump for lump, rent for rent on either side. On its left a vast wound, partly calloused, partly smashed, partly rotted, cleft the wood showing where, at some timeless distance, an accident of massive proportion had befallen the tree causing much of its bulk to fall away. A lightning strike, a huge and violent wind? This immeasurable damage might have been caused by either of these things.

But the tree had survived. Its right side had continued to grow and flourish. A secondary trunk of ponderous immensity sprang out, rising stoically to a jagged top. This had itself given rise to a near horizontal lateral branch to which time had also added size. This vast branch travelled for eight or ten feet before soaring upwards again towards the sky. From this lateral and its adjoining leader the bulk of the living foliage grew. Somewhere in the fork a black tangle of witches broom gave a dark and sombre appearance.

The tree was a savage totem to the wild gods of the forest. In the storms of autumn and winter the great superstructure swayed and rocked but its ossified timbers always bore the strain. The stiffened fibres twisted and groaned and the tree uttered deep, tortured cries as if in agony, bemoaning its age.

In spring and summer the tree displayed a softer image. The ground beneath it became an inviting bed of soft plants and grasses liberally sprinkled with the crisp litter of acorns and bud scales and interminable strippings detached from the upper branches. The bracken held back and there was a beckoning glade here beneath the monarch.

It was this gentle scene that the James family saw as they motored through the Forest towing their caravan.

An Indian summer was moving gently into a painted autumn. The Forest was in primal beauty. Victor James, his wife and their young family were enjoying their holiday tour through the Welsh Marches. They turned off from the Wye Valley to see the Forest of Dean. Motor caravanning was in its early days. Camping sites were few and far between and there was an informality about this form of touring which provided its great attraction.

Evening was approaching and the James's looked for a convenient place to pull over and spend the night. Suddenly they saw it. There, not many yards from the road and beneath a great tree of immense proportions was a clear, dry space which would accommodate both caravan and car.

The children cried simultaneously - *"There it is, Dad. Perfect!"*

Mr James laughed in agreement and swung the rig gently off the road into the space beneath the oak.

It took just a minute to unhitch the caravan, put down the jacks.

"Made for it," said Victor. The kids were already running screaming amongst the adjacent trunks, hiding in the bracken, leaping and dancing with glee.

Mrs James's mother accompanied the family as an additional carer. *"Victor, you take the kids for a romp. Mother and I will get a meal together,"* said Victor's wife bustling into the small galley.

"Good idea," said Victor and ran after the nearest child with growls and roars like a wild animal.

Victor could see clearly all the way back to the caravan. It stood there underneath the spreading branches of the oak. The scene was tranquil and untroubled. No person or beast moved in the woods. An occasional car cruised along the main road. He waited for his wife or his mother-in-law to come to the open door of the van to signal the meal was ready.

A small wind arose rustling the foliage. It increased in sudden boisterous gusts tossing the higher sprays and causing the branches of the oak to sway ponderously. But there was no sign of rain and the James's played on.

Mrs James had just added the hot water to the dehydrated mashed potatoes (she found them the most convenient on tour). Sausages simmered in the pan and a saucepan of baked beans awaited dishing up.

Suddenly, and without warning, the caravan responded like a drum to a savage blow seemingly dealt to its panelling from somewhere outside! It was not a sharp blow such as might have been produced from a rock thrown or from a falling branch. It had power and weight and a certain amount of muffled density. The metal panelling responded, shuddering and resonating, small objects in the van echoed the force of the impact.

Mrs James's mind groped for an explanation. This was not easily arrived at on the spur of the moment. One of the children dashing at the van, arriving with hands outstretched would not have produced an effect as grand as this, but seemed rational. Had Victor with his greater weight stumbled against the side? No, she could see through the window, Victor and both the children played innocently some distance away. They seemed unaware of the problem. She went outside and did a circuit of the van. No broken branch lay on the ground; no living thing ventured nearby or afar!

Mrs James frowned and said to her mother, *"That was most odd! I thought the children might be playing tricks."*

Her mother looked alarmed and enquired, *"No-one - nothing about?"*

"Not a thing."

"Could it have been a stag bolting?" Her mother's voice was shaky. It seemed absurd but who knew what the behaviour of wild forest creatures could be? Mrs James had mental pictures of mad stags stampeding through the forest.

"Don't be silly, Mother." She added rather weakly, "We'd've seen it, wouldn't we?"

Mother looked uneasy.

The next thunderous blow really upset the women. Mrs James rushed to the door. *"Victor!"* she screamed. *"Whatever 's going on out there?"*

Victor waved happily, totally unaware of the crisis at the van. *"Come on kids. Your mother's calling us in for food."*

They were hungry. The clan gathered speedily and ran towards the van.

The white faces of he women told Victor something was wrong. They crowded up the steps.

"Whatever is the matter?"

"Someone's playing tricks with us! Someone out there is banging the van!"

"There's no-one out there. Not a soul."

"Must be. They're running off and hiding."

"Listen Dora. I"ve been watching all the time. There's no-one about. I could not have missed them." Victor's voice was calm and reassuring.

"Well, I tell you something strange is happening, isn't it Mother?"

"Yes - an awful banging on the outside of the van."

Victor dashed out and did a quick circuit of the van. It was still light and so he had no trouble. He shouted vainly towards the trees, *"Anyone out there?"*

All was completely silent except for sighing of the rising wind.

Victor returned. His expression was of puzzlement. The children looked from one face to another waiting for the inevitable explanation.

But it did not come. Instead the van shuddered under a tremendous blow which shook it to its very chassis.

Victor dashed out once more seizing the jack handle as he went. But the area was blank and apart from the rustling of the leaves quite soundless.

They all now looked from one pale face to another. No word was said until Victor volunteered, *"Well, the obvious thing to do is to move on,"* he paused, *"- to somewhere undisturbed."*

"Yes," said his wife, *"let's go now."* She set down the pan of partly mixed mashed potato which she had somehow continued to grip.

Victor, hitched up the car and mobilized the caravan. Within ten minutes they were drawing out from beneath the oak feeling a sense of relief to be moving on along the road. Hardly a word was spoken.

A small inn appeared as they rounded a bend.

"Let's go and have one to steady our nerves," breathed Victor. There was no dissent.

The bar was practically empty because it was still quite early in the evening. Yes, the children would be alright so long as they sat still and behaved themselves. It was still of the era when minors were not allowed by law into public licenced premises. But in the country there was some tolerance.

Victor collected the drinks, a pint of bitter for himself, a sherry for his wife, a gin and tonic for his mother-in-law and red pop for each of the children.

"Holiday?" enquired the landlord, a burly, florid-faced man with thin, greasy hair.

"Yeah. Touring," said Victor taking a welcome gulp at his beer. *"We've got a caravan."*
He paused. *"You couldn't direct us to a satisfactory site where we might spend the night, could you?"*

The publican sucked his teeth. *"The paddock by the pub is mine. You could stay there the night if you don't mind the sheep. Use the toilets in the morning - that is if you give me a bit of trade this evening."*

Victor looked over at his wife who was listening to the conversation. She nodded vigorously. Victor felt the tension receding. It was as if a load had been lifted from them.

"We'll take you up on that kind offer, landlord, if we may. And in fact, if you do any sandwiches or snacks we'd like to order some. We were about to prepare our meal a little way back along the road when we were disturbed - by strange circumstances - and I'm sure the ladies are a bit too put out to want to start another meal."

"Surely," said the landlord. *"It will have to be something fairly simple like cheese an' pickle or eggs or something like that."*

"Fine," said Victor. *"Cheese sandwiches sounds good but anything you've got most of."*

"Right, sir," said the landlord and disappeared in the direction of the kitchen. In a few seconds he returned. *"The wife's got that in hand."*

"Have you had some trouble, sir? You all looked a bit shaken when you came in."

Victor hesitated. He did not want to appear foolish. *"Well, we did have a curious experience just back down the road a little way on the edge of the forest. We pulled in there - ."*
" - under an enormous oak tree," finished the landlord.

"Why yes!" said Victor with considerable surprise. *"It seemed just the spot - a sort of natural place just big enough for the van and the car. Idyllic and all that."*

The landlord was was sucking his teeth. *"And you thought somebody was a-thumping on the van. Playing tricks perhaps. But there was no-one about?!"*

"Right! But how did you know?!"

"Well sir. Your experience is not unique. It happens several times each season. They all come here for a stiff one afterwards!"

He paused. *"There is an explanation - but you'll hardly believe it."* He shot a dramatic glance at Victor.

He went on.*"That tree is old, as you can imagine. Very, very old. Five hundred years old some do say. Now you will know too that hereabouts in the Forest of Dean was a sort of skirmishing ground between the Cavaliers and the Roundheads during the Civil War."*

"Bit long ago, isn't it?" interjected Victor.

"Yes, but I'll make the connection in due course," continued the landlord. *"The Royalists was based at Goodrich and the Parliamentarians was at Gloucester. Both of them was in the habit of sending out skirmishing parties into the Forest. They gave each other no quarter when they met and there was some nasty incidents hereabouts. The few people living in the Dean was not really on anybody's side. But they did hate Sir John Winter, a Royalist who had owned most of the Forest and didn't really give a toss for those who lived there."*

Victor and his family were now all ears. But they had no idea how their recent incident linked up with these details about the Civil War and its protagonists.

The landlord paused for a while.*"You pulled your rig up right under that old tree, didn't you say?"*

"Yes," said Victor. *"You're right. Right underneath it"*

The landlord looked at Victor's near empty glass. *"Another sir?"*

"Yes, of course."

"The ladies?"

Victor's mother-in-law held out her glass. Her eyes were popping out of her head. Mrs James shook her head. The children demanded more pop.

The landlord filled Victor's glass at the pump and the gin from the optic. He deftly tore the cap from a tonic bottle on the opener at the edge of the counter.

He went on. *"It seems back in 1650 or thereabouts, a foraging party of the King's men from Goodrich Castle rode out to the village - such as it was, and that was not very much - looking for supplies. On the road they came upon an old Forester driving a pig. Needless to say they stopped him, said they were commandeering his pig. They demanded to know where there was more. The old man spat and gave a rude answer which greatly upset the officer in charge.*

"'Ye old reprobate,' he cried. 'He who spits on me spits on the King,' and with that he draws his cutlass and hamstrings the Forester. The old man falls to the ground but is unrepentant. 'Ye defile the King with your presence,' he screams. 'Ye ugly, unwashed curs. Begone back to your den!'

"'Oho! We have a jackanapes here,' snarls the officer, an' he leaps off his horse and straddles the old man who spits and lashes out while the officer sits astride him.

"'Sieze his arms,' shouts the officer and two of his three men jump down and spreadeagle the old chap's arms pinning him to the ground.

"'Right ye unspeakable eater of swine dung', shouts the officer in fury, pulling out his dagger. "I'll teach you some manners!" and with that he prizes out both the old man's eyes with the point of his blade!

"The screams of the old man can be heard in the village.

"'Hang him,' commands the officer and without more ado the troopers hoist the old man to his feet, throw a rope over a big branch of the oak, and haul him up.

"But before they get the noose to his neck, the old man curses them. 'Ye'll never get back to the Castle', he cries. 'Death and destruction will befall you - every man of you!'

On the road they came upon an old Forester driving a pig.

"'Get him up,' snarls the officer and the troopers haul the poor old chap up and leave him to gurgle his last moments.

"'Leave him there as an example,' commands the officer."

Victor and his family are now listening boggle-eyed.

The publican has paused dramatically, waiting for the significance of his story to register.

"The noise! - The bangs! - You mean....!" Victor stutters.

The publican's eyes narrow and stare into Victor's. *"That's right - the bangs on your caravan was the shade of the old man's corpse as the rising wind caused it to swing. You see, you were parked directly under that big horizontal branch which the troopers used to hang him from! You were in his space. His astral body still hanging there, swings when the wind gets up! In his agony that poor old chap's soul had become welded to that of the tree."*

Victor was now speechless. Surely it could not be. Yet there was no other explanation.

"The story of the old man who had his eyes put out by Royalists is recorded in history." The landlord sucked his teeth.

Victor looked round at his family all shocked by what they had heard.

"Well, there's more things in Heaven and Earth than meets the eye," declared his mother-in-law.

"Let's go back!" cried the kids in unison.

"Not on your Nellie!" voiced Mrs James.

"There's a sequel," said the landlord.

"Really," said Victor. *"We must hear it."*

"The troopers slaughtered the pig. But you ought to remember this pig was not like the prime specimens you see today. It was more like a wild animal with a long snout and covered in coarse hair. It was a sow.

"Well, there's this poor old Forester having choked his last and this dastardly bunch of Cavaliers thinking they might as well get on home to Goodrich. At least they've got the pig and they've had a bit of sadistic sport with a recalcitrant Forester. As they winds their way through the Forest towards Howle Hill there's a mighty crashing in the undergrowth and this giant wild boar dashes out. It's no weakling. As big as a donkey and ten times more ferocious than a bull mastiff, it gores the officer's horse which rears and throws him. His foot catches in the stirrup and the horse rolls on him just far enough to crush his pelvis. He screams in agony. The troopers jump down and drag him clear. He's in a bad way his legs crushed and twisted and his pelvis about half its normal width, the bones protruding through his hips. The boar has gone as mysteriously as it appeared.

"The troopers cut some poles and lash them together to make a crude litter. They load the stricken officer into this and in order to stop it bouncing around too much, they load also the carcass of the pig which in turn they lash to the officer. They have to shoot the officer's horse, its belly is ripped open and its guts spilling out after the huge boar had done with it. One trooper drags the litter behind his horse. They are badly handicapped. They move on towards the Wye Valley. The officer is conscious and in enormous pain. He curses and screams in delirium. Their passage can be heard far and wide through the vert.

"As they descend towards the valley they are intercepted by a large party of Roundhead skirmishers. The Cavaliers try to run but are overtaken. A Roundhead rides up to the trooper with the officer and pistols him through the head. He falls off. The horse bolts dragging the lurching swaying officer screaming in agony as his broken bones grind together. The horse heads for the river. It overshoots the steep bank and plunges down into the stream. The officer has slipped sideways but is still bound to the pig. The horse reaches the other side by a miracle. When it emerges from the water the officer's corpse has disappeared together with that of the pig. He has drowned.

"The remaining two troopers do not stand a chance. They are seized. This is a war in which no quarter is given. Two burly Roundheads pinion them while a third slits their throats.

"The old man's last curse has come true.

The Cavaliers never got home."

*There are those who may question this story. But the incident at Drybrook is mentioned in Nicholls. **

The inn in the story? In the absence of the fictitious James's of course, it did not exist. But speculation is sweet. It might have been The Hawthorns - long since closed and unique in having a bar divided by the County borders of Hereford and Gloucester and where, according to legend, drinkers moved from one end to the other when the closing times in the two Counties were at odds! It might on the other hand, have been the New Inn at Rudge. Or it may have been one or other of the many inns in Drybrook which, since the war, have gradually closed. Drybrook, like many other regions in the Forest, has a rich heritage in inns.

There were many great oaks in the Forest that survived the storm of 1662. Among them Jack of the Yat and the Newland Oak were especially famous. Little if anything of them remains today.

Some say the Hanging Oak of my story, was near the old Buttonshank Pit. Others say it was farther over near the Deep Cutting. Some claim it was shattered by the freeze of 1962/63. Many Forest oaks were decimated by the weight of snow and ice which formed on their branches. They literally split asunder.

** Nicholls's Forest of Dean. Page 36*

Acknowledgements

My debt to old friends and acquaintances who, in so many ways I have drawn upon in compiling this book is beyond calculation. Many of these friends have, perhaps unconsciously, contributed inspiration merely by being my friends. Some have passed on out of the idyllic green world to which their presence added such an inherent part; remembering them is important.

Many still alive, have extended their goodwill and their support in my having used their names and names of their families and loved ones.

Other sources are less personal but provide the bedrock of what we in the Forest call our traditional heritage.

Firstly there are all my workmates who were *"in the woods"*, employed by the Crown. In particular there are Derek and Dave Cinderey, Ray Jones, Reg and Cyril Wall, Tom Cinderby, Ernie Gibbs, Cliff Phelps, John Brain, Stan East, Joe Cook, Gilbert "Farmer" Brain and his two sons Bert and Ron, the Jones' brothers Dick, Frank, Fred and Sid, Cyril Jones and many more. There is George Lees and his daughter Betty.

From earlier days there are John Smart, Jim Hale, Des Bower, Hedley Morgan, Don Wild and a host of others who attended Steam Mills School in the 1930s.

More formally there are Mabel Beech, Ron Smith's family, the Jehovahs' Witnesses, Sister Celestin of St Anthony's Convent, Humphrey Phelps, John Hosking. Ken Gibbs, grandson of Ernie. Mrs. Stan East. George Cinderby. The lady who once lived at Varnister Farm. Philip Thomas.

For source information there has been H G Nicholls's *Forest of Dean* and *Iron Making in the Olden Times*, David Bick's *The Old Industries of Dean*, Frank Harris's *The Wyntours of Whitecross*, Ralph Anstis' *Four Personalities from the Forest of Dean*, Leonard Clarke's *Who Killed the Bear*, F W Harvey's poem Warning, A H Smith's *English Place Names in Gloucestershire*, publications by the Forest of Dean Newspapers, the proceedings of the Royal Forest of Dean and the Yorkley Angling Clubs.